Small Town
SECRETS

HARLOW SERIES BOOK FOUR

KATERINA SIMMS

One

LAILA KILLED the engine to her car, her eyelids heavy and her limbs aching from another overnight shift at Marston's 24-hour grocery store. The time on her dash said 7:07am and a pale morning light crested the roof of her modest two-bedroom rental up ahead. Meanwhile, her heart lurched because she had less than a few hours to catch a nap, then study, before her mother came by with Whitney, Laila's daughter.

She reached for the door handle and a dash of white caught her eye through her side mirror, a moving van slowing to a stop in the driveway next door. Two men jumped out and a midnight blue SUV pulled over at the sidewalk.

"Now, who's this?" she whispered to herself, her voice croaky from her hours at work.

She pushed her door open and slid out of her old Suzuki sedan, standing still amidst the chilled air and simply observing as the door to the SUV cracked open.

That's when *he* stepped out. Her new neighbor. At least that's what the moving van strongly suggested. Tall and handsome, with dark hair, and equally swarthy features. He held a neutral expression that was mostly unreadable. His shuttered air made him seem instantly too worldly for a place like Harlow, Minnesota. A place where most failed to hold any secret close.

Including her.

If I had more money, I'd be outta this town like a shot...

Any outsider would describe this small town as sweet and idyllic. Any outsider who didn't know that a crime syndicate fast made its mark on every resident here. Heck, just six weeks ago her own sister, Ally, had been taken hostage amidst a bloody showdown in some nearby empty field. There'd been gunshots and henchmen, and there was no telling if or when the syndicate would be back. Soon, her new neighbor here would know all this too.

Her mind cleared enough to register her mysterious stranger staring back at her, his dark eyes narrowing slightly and sending a sharp jolt through her body. Though she'd been looking less *at* him, more *through* him—her thoughts pinging between who he might be and whether he actually knew what he was getting into moving in here —none of that mattered now. She'd been caught staring.

She chastised herself for being so careless, not a trait she indulged in all that often. Especially when it came to who she looked at in public, where usually, she didn't "look" at all.

Through the loud thrum of her heartbeat, she tried to play casual by focusing on the men unloading the van, as if they were *far* more interesting than the dusky guy she *hadn't* been half-checking out. The men moved efficiently, rolling a modest white couch on its side on a hand dolly, the wheels rattling from the truck bed and down the uneven ramp to the ground. An awful lot of noise for a woman who just wanted to catch some sleep.

This could take a while...

The men entered the house, and she shook her head. For some inexplicable reason she sensed her neighbor's attention still on her and she glanced at him strolling past the truck and toward his house. The entire time, she tried not to think too much about why she found this newcomer so intriguing, pinning her interest on his newness and the fact that he seemed so out of place. Either way, her opinion on this man didn't matter. Before long Whitney would be back and Laila would have more than enough to keep her busy.

Wanting to avoid any connection, she snapped her gaze away and pretended not to care about her new neighbor's actions. Instead, she hurried over her aged porch steps and inside the house she worked so endlessly to afford. Speaking of endless work, she was still exhausted and needed to rest, at least for a little while before she dug into her homework for the extra summer classes she had to pass in the next month if she wanted to graduate her sonography degree early.

She needed to graduate. And she needed to do it by year's end. So, she could have more money and more hours to spend with her kid, a kid growing up way too fast. Time was not Laila's friend here, but at the age of twenty-six, she'd eventually dig herself out of the hole she'd fallen into four years ago. Things would start to look up. They had to.

Whitney would get her mom back.

Laila could lose her guilt.

She'd finally give her child the stability she always dreamed of providing, before misplaced trust and single motherhood left her minus any money or bankable skills.

The front door now open, she trekked across her living room's aged, beige carpet, her faded brown couch with cushions that sagged situated on her left. She dumped her purse on a matching worn armchair and pushed on down the hall and into her bedroom. There, she changed into some comfortable cotton loungewear and then threw herself onto her queen-sized mattress with a *humph*.

Not much more than a few minutes passed before her eyelids fluttered closed and she drifted to sleep. Though the delirium of dreamland made nailing down any real clear thought impossible, images of the mystery man next door played on her mind and startled her awake.

Or maybe it was the remnants of a loud knock at her front door lingering on her brain. She couldn't quite delineate what was real and what wasn't, but she jolted to sitting either way. Maybe all the weird desperation and fatigue of recent years had her wishful thinking...

The discordant colors between her aqua blue clock on her lemon-yellow wall spoke of the "joys" of renting. She had little say on wall color or aged carpet, but at least the clock worked, and little more than forty-five minutes had passed during her nap. Now that she was awake, she might as well hit the books. Aside from Whitney returning soon, Emilia Bonacci's and Blaine Callaghan's wedding was happening tomorrow, which just added more tasks to Laila's list of things to do today. Though at least the wedding would be a rare day out for her and Whitney. *They don't get enough of those.*

Before she could even stand, another knock came, and this time, definitely real and from her front door.

"Shit." She ground the expletive under her breath and ran a palm over her hair, still tied in her work ponytail and likely a mess. After a few seconds, she strode across her house and tried to fully awaken from her insufficient sleep, even as she wrenched the front door open, falling short of barking out an abrasive, *"What do you want?"*

And the reason she fell short?

He stood there.

All tall, dark, and handsome, in a beaten-up-and-rugged sort of way. As much as she tried not to, she once more couldn't hold back from staring. This time, the slight pull of his black t-shirt over visibly strong and broad chest muscles caught her, along with the indisputably beautiful golden glow of his thick arms peeking out from that shirt. *Latino. He must be Latino.* In a town that failed at diversity, he most definitely *would* stand out!

At least, he does to me. And in all the ways I wish he didn't....

Catching her mental lapse on his beauty, she jerked her attention up to his face and the mild imperfection of shallow lines scoring his forehead. Even the slight flaws in his skin somehow added character and damning appeal.

And he hasn't even spoken one word yet....

Oh, get your brain together!

Right, she, of all people, understood the pitfalls of impulse and hormones. Especially with a man such as this. The amused glimmer in his eye said he likely had far too much good fortune with women. That glimmer said she'd already given away too much of her inner thoughts.

Though her cheeks burned with embarrassment, she conjured the reminder that she was a realist. She *had* to be. Her child's well-being relied on her mother's clear thought and careful planning. As did

Laila's battered heart. So, being realistic, she thought about how she had every reason to stay away from any man of dating age. How she'd just come off a long shift at her cruddy job. How she'd just woken and probably looked like a flaming hot mess. How *this* man would never give her a second thought if not for whatever reason that brought him to her doorstep now.

"Hi"—she cleared the gravelly tone from her throat and swept another hand over her frazzled hair—"what do you need?"

"I'm sorry to bother you." Adrian Ramos extended a hand to his new neighbor, her striking cornflower blue stare skating over him, while she failed to take hold of his hand. "My name's Adrian, but most people call me by my last name, Ramos. I'm moving in next door and…"

He nodded down to his hand, reminding her that she should shake it. Her gaze dropped, acknowledging his hint and still failing to act on the offer, her attention bouncing up again, while her eyes narrowed in on him. "Ramos? As in, Dean's friend who kidnapped Sarah?"

His heart sank from disappointment that his reputation preceded him. Though she was technically correct about him kidnapping Sarah Overton, this woman omitted the huge detail of *why* he'd done that.

"I was doing Dean a favor, infiltrating the syndicate." He took his hand back and shifted his focus from the purple shadows under this woman's eyes to the overgrown lawn gracing her front yard. She seemed overwhelmed and maybe coming over to introduce himself had been a mistake. "I likely saved her life."

"Right."

He turned back at the sound of her flat tone, yet another thing to leave him wondering if he'd imagined the burst of chemistry they'd exchanged across driveways just an hour earlier. "That's also why I'm back in town. To help with curtailing the syndicate once again."

And even as doubt brought heaviness to his stomach, a light tingling within his chest said he wasn't wrong about that earlier spark and that he still liked what he saw.

Trying to decipher the emotions dancing across her face, he paused to inspect her some more. From a distance, and before coming to this door, he'd thought she might offer the potential for some light fun during his stay in town. Someone to keep him company, since his whole schtick of being an investigator for hire meant never staying still or in one job for too long. But her gaze no longer skittered away like before, so perhaps this nameless woman wasn't the sort to toy with, after all...

She lifted her lips into an all-too-perceptive smile, a dimple on her left cheek seeming to suggest that she sensed a shift in power here. "So, again, did you need something, or are you just stopping by to say, 'Hi'?"

Her direct question warned him not to do his usual act of flirting his way into a woman's world, but more the fool to her, because he was used to risk and liked a challenge. Even if the odds were stacked firmly on him losing.

"I *do* need something." He shifted his gaze past her and into her house, to the worn-but-homely carpet and furnishings, to a kitchen table stacked with a basket of unfolded laundry on one end and a backpack next to a pile of books on the other.

A student, maybe?

She looked to be in her mid-twenties, a little older than the usual college age, but then, maybe that explained why she'd hauled out of her car earlier wearing some kind of retail worker's uniform under her jacket.

A student *and* a night shift worker.

"I've come a long way and was hoping to buy some groceries soon." He blinked and then re-focused on her, making sure to flash a smile and lean in a little closer. "Only, my power is off until this afternoon and I was hoping to run an extension cord from your house to my fridge?"

She dipped her chin, already hinting that he asked too much. "And you can't wait a few hours 'til the power's on?"

He shrugged. "A man's gotta eat."

He took in her slow and pensive breaths, not sure why he stuck on talking to her. It wasn't like he needed the distraction, or anymore ties to this place, or anyone the syndicate might connect to him as leverage. He'd come here to protect his friends and could already feel the syndicate closing in. And still...

Maybe this fish out of water life is taking its toll...

Right. He'd lived in all sorts of places: army barracks, deserts, foreign villages, and bustling cities like L.A. where he'd grown up. But never an endearing little town such as Harlow. He didn't belong here. In a community cozier than anything he was used to. Maybe that explained the tight skepticism across this woman's face, even as she released the tension from her shoulders and spoke, "I mean, it's probably not all that safe to string up cords across houses, what if it rains and—"

"It's mid-summer. There's no rain forecast for today." He gave another easy shrug, though his shallow breaths showed that ease to be a lie. "I checked."

The woman's expression remained firm and unconvinced, especially as she gave her eyes a quick roll to the heavens. "I'm not letting you into my house."

Now it was his turn to unleash a deadpan tone. "Scared I'll kidnap you too?"

"And take me away from all this?" She gestured to her house, granted, a bit more than rundown. "Oh, please, do."

Though her lips pressed into a thin and sarcastic line, a short and buried laugh jolted the space just below his ribcage. Still, he found a new way to use the quip about her house to motivate her toward enduring his presence for a few minutes more. "I'll pay you for your trouble."

No sooner had he pulled out and opened his wallet, then she shot out a hand and snatched out a crisp fifty.

"There's an outlet along the outside wall there, facing your house." She stabbed her thumb in some vague direction to her left. "I'm sure you'll find it easily enough."

Here he'd been, hoping to win her trust, only to question her doubts about having him inside her house. He'd never needed to be "in her house." Not with an outdoor outlet, anyway.

Maybe she just doesn't like you, Asshole.

Could he even find fault in her money-swipe when he was just as bad for using cash to coax her? Also, he was in Harlow to do a job, so maybe her curt approach served him well after all.

With every passing second with this strange new neighbor, he found himself questioning his past assumptions on small town hospitality. And with every question, he found himself even more intrigued to know what her deal was.

"Thanks." He made sure his short expression of gratitude dropped hard like a lead balloon, the strain taking over his body only easing as he observed more details.

The tuft of messy hair sticking out from her ponytail. A tuft not there during his first glimpse of her on her driveway…

"Oh." He honed in on the light indented lines over her left cheek. "I woke you?"

Her brows bowed, like she didn't understand, so he pointed to the lines on her face. "You have pillow marks right there."

She startled back a step, blinking and pressing a palm to her cheek, her pupils wide like him noticing her fatigue left her mortified.

Why? Why would she want to hide being tired?

He nodded and made sure to soften his expression, exchanging his earlier forced gratitude for something more genuine. "I'm sorry. I'll get out of your way."

"No!" Though breathy, she dropped her hand and her brows dipped again, denoting confusion. "It's okay."

Now her lips bent as though she maybe hadn't meant to be so forgiving, though the softened tension over her cheekbones said she second-guessed that reaction too. "Laila. My name's Laila."

A long and heavy pause held while they stared at each other, the dart of her gaze seeming to question everything about this moment, perhaps none more so than why she even offered her name. She'd been reluctant just moments earlier.

To be fair, he couldn't figure it out either, except to say that for some reason, his observation on her napping seemed to throw her. That said, he knew enough people who didn't like to admit they were human. Her reaction wasn't wholly unusual, except that he was more used to that reaction from battle and street roughened men. Not some sweet seeming lady living in a quiet, country town.

No doubt this one has a story…

But he'd asked far too much already, so he gave a small nod and stepped back, already walking away as he spoke one last time. "Nice meeting you, Laila. I'll see you around."

Two

ROCHELLE FERRARA PULLED her hire car over outside the welcoming orange lights of Maynard's Tavern, lights that failed to brighten the anxiety that kept her body stiff all over.

Just thirty minutes earlier, she'd stood out front of the large wooden sign belonging to Harlow's one and only B&B, suitcase in hand, the establishment not at all what she'd expected. First off, a handwritten note taped to the door stated that the aging building was *Under New Management*. Second, the door in question had been *locked!*

No entry for her. Or anyone else with a booking. Not that there'd been anyone else around. Not even the door's note offered any further explanation. Not a phone number to call. Nor did the one listed in the email from her initial booking work.

Trying her best to restrain her frustration and panic, she'd returned to her car, then sat there staring at the circular Mercedes badge for a quiet moment, only to realize her car commented on her wealth and made her stick out, and therefore made her feel even more vulnerable. She had nowhere to go. No one to call. She was stranded.

The only person she knew in town was Emilia Bonacci, and she wasn't about to bother her on the eve of her wedding. An attempted internet search showed slow network coverage, followed by literally no other places that might take a last-minute weekend booking. That's when she'd seen Maynard's Tavern listed as a place of interest. She'd passed the venue on her way into town, had noted its heavenly lights....

Now, heart heavy, she pushed her car door open and approached the large venue—one stranded at the edge of a giant and empty paddock, but her best bet at this late hour.

Despite all hope, a quick glance through the front window showed no customers conversing at tables and no music was heard playing through the glass.

What if there's no one inside?

Still, she pushed at the weighty wooden door and the thing surprisingly swung open. A warm atmosphere engulfed her on entry, complete with dim lights and old-style furnishings that melted a portion of the strain compressing on her chest.

She took a deep breath and stepped toward the bar. After a decade in high-end furniture dealing, she could tell her oak from her ash wood, rococo from art deco, and right now she took in the details of bentwood chairs tucked under mid-century style, square timber tables, along with mahogany-brown leather booths filling the spaces along the sidewalls. Indeed, no other customers remained, and the tavern did seem closed, but even as her heart sank, she clung to the small positive detail that the door had been unlocked.

Just as she reached the bar, a tall figure caught her eye in the tucked away kitchen behind the food service counter. A man wiping down a stove. Far too busy to notice her.

She leaned into the bar, the protruding edge digging into her torso, as she called out, "Excuse me."

The man turned his shaved head, and she made out the details of a full face, with pale blue eyes narrowed like he hadn't expected anyone to be around, and he sought to discern who she might be. A slight ridge between his brow denoted a moment of annoyance before his expression relaxed altogether.

"Just one minute."

He dropped the cloth to a counter and strode toward her, through a swinging door to the bar's right, before stopping behind the bar proper. Even as he stood before her, he said nothing more. Less rude, more... confused... Maybe?

She sank back onto her black Fendi heels and donned an air of confidence she'd long learned to wear in moments of uncertainty. "Are you open?"

The man behind the bar smiled but shook his head.

"No, dear." Despite his bleak reply, the warmth in his voice extended to his eyes in an odd mix of joy and sympathy that melted something within her. "Just closing up, though I thought Sarah would've locked the front door on her way out."

The ridge between his brows appeared again, as though he pondered "Sarah's" mistake. Meanwhile, Rochelle dropped her gaze to the bar's dark woodgrain, her wood-gazing having more to do with a desire to delay an ever more inevitable night in her car.

Just twenty-four hours earlier she'd been sipping perfectly brewed espresso on the cobbled streets of Florence, Italy. She'd just cut a deal with a renowned local dealer to add some of his antiques for sale to her list of wealthy clients.

The trip had encompassed everything she loved—travel back to her family's homeland, hours upon hours immersed in classic art, amazing food, and a chance to grow her business, only now....

"Ohh..." The unexpected, deflated sound fell from her lips, but she half-turned away all the same, not wanting to bother this man anymore.

"Do you need help, Love?" His endearing question caught her midstride and his continued words had her turning back his way. "I'm Gordon, the chef here. Is there something I can do?"

The strain in her shoulder blades eased and a small sense of relief washed over her. "I'm in town for Emilia's wedding, and I was hoping to at least stay the weekend for an overdue break from flying about, but now Harlow's one and only B&B is closed indefinitely, and my booking is seemingly canceled. I don't have anywhere to go." She cringed, trying to make light of her situation, while very little within her felt light. "As it stands, I'll be spending tonight in my car."

"Hmmm..." Gordon gave a small and repeated nod, his lips

pressed into a thoughtful thin line. "Well, I'm sure it's not as bad as that. You eaten lately?"

She shook her head. "I've come here straight from the airport, but—"

"Alright then." He reached across the bar and patted her hand, his touch and instant acceptance rocking her more than if he'd simply sent her away. "We'll feed you and figure out the other details as we go. How does that sound?"

Incredulous laughter burst past her lips. Just like that, he'd help her? She lifted her gaze to his heart-melting smile, one that stole any questions over how quickly he was willing to put himself out to make her life easier. Even more confusing, the longer she looked at him, the more she liked what she saw. Even more appealing than his looks was the ease of his demeanor and his unassuming kindness.

Is this country hospitality or is there something else at work here?

Do I mind either way?

A slow smile tugged at her lips, and for some inexplicable reason, she turned her hand and clasped on to his. "I'll cut you a deal, Mr. Gordon. You let me into that kitchen back there, and I'll cook us both a meal."

His smile shifted from amused at her address of "Mr. Gordon" to slight suspicion at her request to use his kitchen, perhaps an understandably territorial man when it came to that space.

But she'd spent her whole life surrounded by powerful and territorial people, so had no qualms about letting go of his hand and powering around the bar toward those swinging doors.

"The name's Rochelle, by the way." She marched on, every step taking her farther and farther away from being stopped. Her jet-setting life offered few chances to cook for herself, when cooking and eating home dishes was what she missed most during her travels. "Hey, were you at the Harlow Fair all those months ago? I swear, you look familiar."

"Ahh... I... I don't know...."

She ignored his uncertain tone and crashed through the double doors, her mood lifting even more at a wood pallet brimming with bunches of fresh herbs, while another contained a small mountain of onions. That said, her first stop was a tall metal shelf holding bottles and bottles of sacred olive oil.

"Oh, yes, I *do* remember you." She turned and beamed at Gordon. "You were serving pulled pork mini burgers at a stall. Best ones I've ever had, by the way."

A pause drew out while his mouth wavered and he seemed to fumble for words, though he did eventually find some. "Yeah, I guess. We did have a stall and I did cook pulled pork burgers, but—"

"Yep, definitely you." She clicked her fingers at him and then thrust a bottle of oil into his hand before he had much time to think. "It's that unexpected, soft Irish lilt of yours. Very charming."

She raised a brow at him and tried not to laugh at his overly still and perplexed stare. "My parents were Irish, but I'm American born and raised. I never figured some of their accent rubbed off on me."

"Maybe it's just that I'm new here and everyone else no longer notices?" She nodded to the oil bottle in his hand. "Now, crack that open for me, will you?"

He peered down to the bottle in his hand, his numb expression lifting to her, while his brow shifted to a firm and heavy set. "Well, hang on a minute, I might have offered to help you, but you can't just traipse in here and take over my kitchen."

She crossed her arms and waited, allowing a few moments of quiet to settle between them. "Okay, so here's my deal"—because cutting deals was what she did best. Because she loved that suspenseful moment where the other person could always say no—"You're right, I am taking over, but I've been on the road for months now and I'd really appreciate a chance to cut loose in this kitchen. I also think you're one attractive man. So, I propose we start with spending some time here cooking together—a recipe of my choice, by the way— and if you're game, you take me home with you tonight."

A rush of adrenaline swept through her body. That she'd been so bold. That she now had her "moment." The one where he could say, "No." Where he could crush her with rejection, though she suspected she'd be less crushed, so much as unfortunate to be at the receiving end of a cold and miserable night in her car.

Everything about this moment carried a distinct weight and silence she wanted to end, though she knew the next opportunity to speak belonged to Gordon.

His cheeks hung a little slack and his mouth slightly open, a low creak preceding his next words. "You mean"—he snapped his mouth shut and took a slow swallow—"as in?"

Sensing he feared elaborating on the question, she took further initiative and dragged her gaze down his body, and then leveled back a sly smile. Maybe Gordon here didn't have a classical heartthrob vibe going on, but she'd been around riches and glamor long enough to appreciate that pure aesthetics weren't everything. She knew how to spot a hidden gem in this man's strong, safe, and sweet demeanor. So, to her, he was downright irresistible.

She shrugged, trying to make her proposition seem as lighthearted and unthreatening as she intended it to be. "You're single, aren't you?"

He gave a slow nod but offered no verbal reply.

So, she spoke again. "Then, why not?"

He blinked again, shaking his head, as if to come to his senses. "You seem so sure I feel the same way about you."

"You don't?" She waited as his gaze did a slow glide down her body, from the low neckline of her figure-hugging black, Dior tank top that displayed a good portion of her full bust, down to the forest green Bottega flare skirt that showcased her unapologetically wide hips.

His focus latched to hers again, wide, and clearly taken aback, before he nodded slowly. "Alright then. We'll give this a whirl."

Three

THE SUN WARMED Laila's face as she tilted her chin up to the canopy of wisteria blooms over the outdoor area at Emilia and Blaine's wedding reception. The Mirabelle River burbled a little farther up ahead. The soft breeze pushed at her Arctic blue tulle dress and she damn-near sighed at how wonderful it felt to just enjoy a rare day out contrary to her usual routine of work, study, and child wrangling—dressed to the nines, and for once feeling human.

Speaking of her child, Whitney whirled on the dance floor with the other little ones inside, giving Laila extra relief from her role of mother. Lively music echoed from the open concertina doors and through to her in the garden, the whoosh of waving wisteria vines and people's chatter melding with the music.

Aggie talked beside her, the table's live flower arrangements a labor of love care of her nursery. And despite Laila's lack of focus, she appreciated the light talk on flower species all the same.

Taking a quick sip from the champagne flute in her hand, she peered down at Aggie and vowed to re-enter the chat. "I have to say, being here sure beats studying or working."

Aggie smiled and deep wrinkles crinkled the skin below her eyes and around her mouth. She reached her age-spotted hand to pat Laila's upper arm and offered a gentle squeeze. "It's been a while since I saw you look so at peace, Dear. It suits you."

Laila tilted her head to one side and tried not to frown at Aggie's observation. "We've all had enough to stress about with the syndicate. You don't need to worry about me, okay? You'll see, just one more year and things will get easier."

She pulled her lips into a confident smile while her tummy muscles turned rigid, and her fingers clasped tighter on the stem of her champagne flute. She'd had years of "not okay" already and couldn't imagine a day when she wouldn't fear having all she'd fought for wrenched away.

A little stunned that her gaze had slipped to the ground, she lifted her attention back to Aggie and sought to convince her once more. Only, her attention didn't land on Aggie so much as veer to the woman's left, where a bronzed god-like man rounded a corner and joined the party.

Ramos?

Oh hell, no! Not him.

She'd thought the sun shone bright before, but the warm glow of his skin outshone anything here, his white dress shirt only adding extra contrast to his "godly" hue. And of course, his every step through the crowd looked more like a dramatic prowl, one that elevated her pulse and stole at her breath.

Though stopped next to Dean, Adrian's dark gaze landed on her, that gaze strong, even as his lips moved in conversation with his friend. She let out a groan but held back from outright rolling her eyes. Whatever she'd planned to say to Aggie faded and she skimmed her attention over the many local women now glancing at Ramos—a new man of dating age always quick to draw attention.

Good! They can have him.

He patted Dean on the shoulder in a clear goodbye and set his stride firmly in her direction.

No. Please. Just no!

She shook her head and flared her eyes, warning him to stay away. Aware that all those *looking* at him would next move to *talking* about him... and by association, *her*. As always, fate chose to be cruel and all too soon he stood at her side, his lopsided grin revealing a way-too-endearing smile.

"Fancy seeing you here." Alongside his baritone voice, his eyes glittered like newly polished onyx.

"It's a small town. I'd say you had a better than fair chance of seeing me." While she clamped her teeth together to keep from saying more, heat rose in her cheeks, that heat making her suddenly aware of how close they stood and that Aggie's never-miss-anything stare clung to them both. "You'll find living in a small town is like that."

Laila shrugged in a "duh" kind of way and she focused on staring into the crowd, making a point of not asking how he'd been, while hoping he and Aggie would maybe get to talking and she could slink away.

"Oh, you've met." Aggie's pitchy delight had Laila squeezing her eyes shut in a doom-filled grimace, but the woman waited until Laila's attention returned, before she spoke again. "Funny things, weddings, dontcha know? What with so much love in the air, some people here are bound to follow the same path as Emilia and Blaine."

She winked at Laila and patted Adrian on his thick bicep, then sauntered away.

While Laila's jaw hung loose, Ramos released a hearty chuckle, which she countered with yet another exasperated groan. So much for her carefree day.

She leveled her stare to him, though the corners of her lips trembled with amusement. "Congratulations. You just got the full Aggie McKey experience. She's about as subtle as a fuchsia ball gown at a funeral."

"Does that bother you?" His smirk grew as though he already knew that Aggie's suggestions *did* bother Laila, but he gave a small shrug and carried on. "Maybe she's got a point."

She scoffed at the way his gaze continued to inspect her, his unwavering focus offering "suggestions" of his own. She shook her head in another denial, her heartbeat thundering, as she pulled her champagne flute higher for another sip. "And maybe you don't know what you're talking about."

"You're right." Again, his eyes glittered, suggesting her rebuffs did nothing to dissuade him, which only made her want to not rebuff him at all. Still, he gestured to the wedding party around them. "I'd ask you to dinner to find out for myself, but it seems Emilia and Blaine saved me the trouble."

"You're assuming I'd say yes." She tilted her head and forced her stare to stay on his face, trying hard not to let her gaze drop to the contours of his body, even though she'd already noticed enough detail there during his walk over. "A little cheap, too." She shrugged, pretending not to care about being rude. "Yah know, since you're technically skimping out on paying for our dinner and letting Emilia and Blaine foot the bill."

He cut loose with another chuckle and pressed a knuckle to his lips, like she truly did break him with her dry and offensive humor. He stepped closer to her—his reaction the exact opposite of what she'd hoped to achieve—while heat emanated from him and transported his dark scent of black pepper mixed with fresh licorice root. "So, you want a man who splashes cash?"

She bit her lower lip and tried to breathe through the perplexing flutter of her diaphragm, with breathing in itself near impossible. "I'm not looking for any man, but if I were, lack of financial stability *would* be a deal-breaker."

She shrugged, unapologetic with her hope that *this* particular man would find her too standoffish and demanding, mostly because she couldn't trust what might happen if he didn't. The man lived directly next door to her, and him *not* being put off would only place more pressure on her to keep a safe distance.

He squinted at her, signaling an awareness of her mind game, before he sucked in a sharp breath and broke his gaze to the people around him. "Financial stability. Got it. Well, I'm thirty-two and have been gainfully employed for about a decade and a half now. I have an exemplary record from my seven-year stint in the US forces, with consistent freelance work in security and investigations ever since." He turned back to her, his flat expression overly bored. "My contracting work has me doing better than all right, and you can chat to Dean, Sarah, or the sheriff if you need references."

His lips pinched upward in a look of smug pride, seeming mostly directed at his ability to call her bluff than any arrogance over his list of achievements or his "references." Meanwhile a searing shiver of unwanted admiration shot up her spine. He was right. On eligibility alone, she had no reason to turn him down.

Shit. I'm never walking outside my front door again.

The shiver turned from hot to cold, as she recalled this man's freedom to move through the world as he wished, while she could do anything but. Certainly not to help any friends, much less dive head-first into the fray of trying to stop a crime syndicate.

No, all her responsibilities and burdens meant she pretty much never had time or money just to take a day off and explore even the next town. So, for all her nit-picking when it came to this man, perhaps she was the one most at risk of letting anyone down.

"That's great." She glanced away and cleared her throat. "Go, you."

Those last words regretfully fell on a choked tone. He must have sensed her despondency because he let the silence hang and didn't press for more conversation.

Well, not until he finally did speak up once more. "So, *would* you like to go out with me sometime?"

Her focus snapped back to him and a half-hearted laugh shuddered past her lips, but only so long as it took for a distinct lump to swell in her throat. She was essentially trapped and could never say yes, and the tight sensation that embraced her ribcage only seemed to support that fact.

She stiffened her expression and gave a resolute head shake, just seconds away from saying that what he wanted and what she could agree to were two absolute polar opposite things.

"Mommy!" Right on cue, Whitney's little voice cut through Laila's stare-off with Ramos, jolting her with a cold shock of reality.

Within seconds, Whit had her arms wrapped around Laila's leg, her wide and excited gaze pinned up high to her mother, her huge grin bringing focus to the light spray of freckles over the crinkled bridge of her nose. She was, of course, gorgeous and completely oblivious to how her sudden presence changed this moment.

Unlike everyone else here, this poor man doesn't know I have a child.

Wanting to delay the inevitable disappointment she would see on Adrian's face; she was slow to lift her attention to his. But even as her gaze did meet his, it seemed she'd still caught his reaction too early for disappointment, his focus darting between Laila and her child. More a look of open surprise.

Bracing for his inevitable cringe of dread, followed by a hurried and mumbled excuse to leave, her heart dropped at what Whitney might see. Her mother being rejected because of her. Though to be fair, she sometimes used Whit's existence to repel unwanted attention from men. Just never, *ever*, in her daughter's presence.

And maybe because Adrian's attention wasn't outright unwanted, his speechlessness now hurt in ways she didn't wish to explore. So, she unpacked reactions she'd performed many other times. *Indifferent.* *Unfazed.* She stiffened her spine, looked him dead in the eyes, and refused to flinch no matter what happened next.

"I tried to warn you. You *don't* know what you're talking about." She shrugged and ticked one corner of her lip higher, exuding and an attitude of, "sucks to be you." Damned if she let this stranger judge her or her child. "It's time for me and *my daughter* to move on."

Four

ADRIAN STOOD DUMBFOUNDED, while Laila powered away, auburn curls bouncing behind her and fingers clasped around her little girl's hand. Until now, he'd had no idea she had a child, and he didn't know how he felt about that.

Hell, forget about the kid. Is she even single?

In his mere twenty-four hours as her neighbor, he hadn't seen any man enter her house. Nor did one seem to be around now. So, maybe he wasn't so off-target there. *But the child?* With Laila's age, he'd assumed... Well, he'd assumed wrong.

He shook his head and used the slow search for his seat at the outdoor wedding area to clear his thoughts. Since his friendship with Dean was common knowledge, he'd start his seat-searching there, his hunch quickly proving correct.

He paused before his chair marked out with his name on a floral card at the table, his focus shifting from the empty seat to his left, and then farther along to a blonde woman he didn't recognize. She wore a long, pale green dress, and had bright blue eyes. Despite her shorter and lighter hair, her features seemed strongly reminiscent of Laila. In a small town such as Harlow, perhaps it wouldn't be a stretch to assume the two were related. A sister. Cousin, maybe?

Just as he settled into his chair and vowed to move on, Laila strode over, defying any expectation she might claim the empty seat beside him and taking the one opposite the blonde. Her daughter was nowhere to be seen, likely back inside dancing with the other kids.

Despite a strong awareness of her presence and the mild tugging in his chest, he made quick with adjusting his position so that his back stayed to her. Meanwhile, a series of low murmurs delivered snippets of the two women's conversation. Something about how they'd visited this site as children. *With their dad.* So, definitely sisters.

Now the chatter livened and moved to how the empty seat next to him was marked for Chip Overton, the blonde's ex, and a name Adrian recalled as the focus of the syndicate's last attack on Harlow. The escalating violence, on top of Dean and Sarah's past ordeal, had pushed Adrian to take up temporary residence in this town.

He caught the blonde's name, Ally—no doubt the same Ally held hostage in the syndicate's recent trap—before he vowed to stop eavesdropping and turned his mind to the glass of wine before him.

Laila's attempts to hide her fatigue yesterday made a lot more sense now. The longer he thought, the more pieces fit together. The late shift she'd returned from. The backpack and books piled on the kitchen table, too big for any little girl no more than four years old. And while Laila and Ally had talked about Chip, there'd been no sign or mention of Laila having a partner.

Then there was her avoidance of being asked out, similar to the same, justified, defenses he'd witnessed as a child from his own mother. A denial of her more human vulnerabilities and needs. As if she could do it all and never require a break. Perhaps like his mother, there was a history of men who bailed whenever the realities of dating a single mom got too much. Though none of that was quite as painful as losing the *one* man with the most incentive to stay. The child's father.

He was also making another huge assumption about why this woman might be single. Perhaps Laila here was a grieving widow. He'd encountered a fair few of those in his years serving. Perhaps she'd never be okay with dating again. With all the uncertainty attached to his job, maybe he'd be best to keep his distance too.

Time to remember why I'm here.

He'd come to this town to help his friend, Dean, and the woman he loved, Sarah—Dean having saved Adrian's ass a number of times in their years serving together overseas. He'd come here to continue his life's work of protecting the vulnerable. To provide extra muscle and the benefit of his contacts and experience in organized crime.

And even as he tried to keep his mind on this mission, Laila too seemed linked to his cause. The gravity of a woman raising a kid alone in a troubled town. What this whole syndicate thing must be to a woman like her, her own sister having already been kidnapped and still a likely target.

He sighed and drew his wine glass closer, aware that Laila didn't seem to be the type to appreciate sympathy or offers of protection. And as much as she probably wouldn't want either of those things, *he* also didn't need any distraction, nor was it in any woman or child's best interest to be linked to him.

Only knuckleheads get attached.

I could never forgive myself if they became a target.

He couldn't make any wrong moves here. He'd have to go slow. Get a better read on this situation. And then maybe retire from the whole "protector" gig forever...

He scoffed into his wine glass and took his first sip, his idea on retiring not bad after all. Even if he did mostly trust his contacts, people under pressure were known to turn. He'd been lucky up until now, maybe too damn lucky. So perhaps he would stop testing his chances and dip out when all this syndicate business ended.

A small voice had him turning back to Laila. Her little girl had approached the table and now tugged at her mother's arm. Once again, she wanted mom back on the dance floor. Laila resisted for a while longer, her focus clinging to her sister as though she held to the last dregs of adult conversation, before she gave in and followed her child.

His attention lingered on her back and his mind wandered to the responsibility and sacrifice someone in her position took on. That thought only held until his gaze dipped to Ally and the scrutiny in her eyes. She'd noticed his staring and clearly had opinions on the matter.

Despite his muscles stiffening at being caught, he raised a brow and challenged her to voice a problem with his interest in her sister. All Ally did was chuckle and shake her head, a pensive expression taking over as she stood. As much as she seemed to want to leave, a man stopped before her, his intense stare spurring Adrian to believe this was the infamous Chip.

Wanting to give these two some space, he found his feet and followed his instincts to Laila on the dance floor. The shock of her having a child had ebbed and he now considered himself capable of talking to her about it.

But he failed to enter the dance floor and instead watched her spin circles with her daughter in her arms. She lifted the child high and kissed her round cheeks, mother and child's laughter rippling out like a gentle wave over his reservations. In spite of having every reason to give this woman her space, a smile out powered his doubts and before he knew it, he pushed his way through the small crowd.

An older woman stepped in his way, her brows and lips set in a firm line. Her prolonged stare held a softer, more concerned edge, one that told him to wait a moment, before she turned and whispered something into Laila's ear.

Laila whipped around, her eyes wide and cheeks hollow, as her gaze landed on him. She hadn't expected him to come back, like she'd assumed having a child would ward him off. And he assumed the woman who'd intervened just now was her mother, which likely only added to Laila's surprise.

The older woman gave him a small nod while she spoke to Laila again, Laila's face hardening as she replied and shook her head. Like her mother wanted her to give him a chance, while Laila seemed firmly against the idea.

She has every reason not to trust me. Likely any man, for that matter.

But the older woman grabbed his hand and jerked him forward, and in the next beat, took Laila's daughter out of her arms and stalked away. As much as he wanted to chase that woman down and thank her, he held back any signs of gratitude so as not to tee-off Laila, instead extending his hand in an offer to dance.

Her stare fixed on his hand for the longest time, making his stomach churn like some awkward kid at prom just waiting for the brutal blow of her rejection. Eventually, her gaze narrowed, and she made eye-contact, the strain over her face quick to ease. "Oh. Fine."

She grabbed at his hand and pulled him in, he chuckled at her abrasive approach and thanked his luck at the current slower music. "Just the sort of enthusiasm I look for in a woman."

She rolled her eyes, but her smiling lips told a different story. "Most guys run the moment they find out about Whitney. What's your deal?"

"You're the one who ran, remember?" Given her reticence and the renewed scowl she pitched his way, as much as he wanted to, he tried not to run a thumb over where his hand connected with her back. Her daughter no doubt meant a great deal to her, and he couldn't imagine the hurt of watching others run away over that same love. "Good people are few and far between, a child and potential ex on the periphery makes no difference. I'd like to find out if you're one of those good people, Laila."

As much as that seemed like an ideal moment to glide closer and claim the benefits of any potential adoration, he stepped back and slid his palms down her arms, taking hold of just one hand and twirling her around. The long hem of her bright blue dress kicked and fanned out, while he tried to not close his eyes and make a show of breathing in the billowing scent of her red apple and jasmine perfume.

Back at center, her gaze latched to his and her brows drew together, her collarbone working up and down as though she were a little breathless. "Lucky for you, exes aren't a problem here."

His world stilled a little as he pondered her statement. Perhaps, like his dad, Laila's ex wanted nothing to do with her and his child. Or perhaps, his previous widow theory applied. Then again, her flat delivery spoke of resentment over grief.

Her brows dipped in a sign she saw his confusion, and she sucked in a breath, before replying, "Whitney's dad went complete incommunicado. I don't even know where he is."

He had to work hard not to belay his anger through tightening his grip around her waist. He knew too well what that kind of abandonment did to a child and their remaining parent. It dented their trust in most people. Especially anyone trying to show romantic interest. That said, he wasn't beyond trying to ease the weigh on this heavier conversation.

"Well, you know where I live, and I have a number you're welcome to call." He offered a "no pressure" sort of smile and slid his hand down to the small of her back, testing her reaction, which turned out to be nothing, and still a heck of a lot better than her slapping him away.

"Real smooth, buddy." In spite of her sarcasm, she huffed out a reluctant laugh and her fingers did an encouraging curl into his shoulders.

The beauty of her deep blue eyes sent a hard pang through his chest. Even her small refusals triggered a protective urge in him. Now that he understood a little more about where her reluctance came from…

"So"—he spoke, but her gaze flittered to her girl sipping at a glass of juice on a barstool next to her grandmother. *This woman worries. A lot.* Not that he could blame her.

He dared to lift his hand and touch the softness of her jawline, bringing her attention back to him again—"How about that dinner? One that's not care of Blaine and Emilia?"

Her lips lifted into a smile, one that added a soft glitter to the rich hue of her eyes, the joy there gone all too soon. "Adrian…"

His name from her lips should have made his heart sing, but the drawn-out dip in her tone only took all hope with it.

She shook her head slowly, only confirming his theories on lost hope. "I work a shitty night job and am studying my proverbial nuts off to graduate early. In between all that, I look after my kid. I don't think you know what you're asking of me here."

"You're wrong about that." He gave a disingenuous shrug, a distinct heaviness dragging at his gut because he could feel her rejection closing in. "I know what I'm asking for. I'm asking for one dinner."

"Okay"—She scoffed and peered down at his chest, still shaking her head as though she figured him one wooly brained fool—"Well, for starters, if you did know, you'd understand that my schedule isn't exactly brimming with free time."

"Because of the kid?" Starting to catch her point now, that this was more about her situation than a dislike of him, his next shrug came a whole lot easier. "Bring the kid with you."

She pressed her lips into a flat line to match her flat stare. "The *kid's* bedtime is seven."

"Fine. Then we'll do lunch."

Though her lips rose into an incredulous smile, her brows bent with seeming skepticism. Just as she opened her mouth to reply—and most likely to turn him down—a random voice called loud across the room. "Hey, everyone. Ally and Chip are fighting over by the river."

The public announcement, over quietly approaching Laila or her mother to defuse the situation, made him wonder if this might be one of those small-town things. You know, a love for anything new and dramatic. That *anyone's* business was implicitly *everyone's* business.

The fact that the other guests' faces lit with glee seemed to confirm his theory.

"Oh, shit." Laila jolted out of his hold and gathered her long hem into her hands, jogging away just as quickly and out the venue's open doors.

Seconds passed before he abandoned his shock long enough to follow her through the outdoor table area and over a large lawn, where a horde of others milled about the party's edge. Though he couldn't hear past the nearby river sounds and people's whispers, Ally stood before Chip crying, her every backward step taking her farther away from the man. Only, Chip drew nearer, his steps faster, as her face lost its hard edge of anger in time for him to pull her into a long and emotionally wrought kiss.

Adrian stood shoulder-to-shoulder with Laila, just as she whispered a breathy, "Wow."

He twisted to find she held one hand pressed to her collarbone, her cheeks pale and slack, like a woman not usually stunned.

Though the crowd clapped and cheered for Chip and Ally's reunion, Laila turned and peered up to him with a resigned sort of shrug. "Still want to ask me out?"

Five

MARK FARRO HUNG up the phone from one of many long conversations with yet another syndicate associate. Once again, he'd had to hash out the implications of his recent setback in Harlow, then graciously accept a new round of reprimands. The words "You fucked up" had become all too familiar and grating to him. After all that was done, he'd shared the news that Rudolph Manzinni was now involved and so this associate—like all other associates—had no choice but to pledge their allegiance to Mark.

He leaned back in his chair and looked out the window of the unsophisticated cabin, in this Podunk town he was forced to hide in. Though not just any Podunk town. This one was in North Dakota, just over the Minnesotan border and not too far from Harlow. A long cry from the hustle and bustle of the cities he enjoyed, but with every syndicate resource at his disposal.

Damn Harlow. No doubt every smug bastard there figured they'd disrupted his plans. And maybe they had. But they hadn't gone nearly far enough. He turned his attention to the thud of footfall and his open office door and the only other person in this cabin. His assistant, Stix. The man strolled past and shot Mark his habitual scowl, then disappeared out of view.

This man had been at his side for years and was the closest person to gain Mark's trust outside of his cousin Luciano, who, thanks to Harlow, still wasted away in a Midwestern prison. But Stix here wasn't very talkative. Not that Mark cared for pointless chatter. Stix's lack of general expression made it impossible to know his thoughts and motivations, which added an air of uncertainty to just *how* much he could be trusted.

One thing Mark did know. Stix had stuck close where others bailed, perhaps under the impression Mark would find them a safe and lucrative exit from the syndicate. But so far, he'd failed. Maybe Mark's mind played tricks, but he got the sense that Stix's low-key seething had increased since landing in this cabin.

With Stix now gone, a chill rippled through Mark's body, and he did something the man had told him not to. He pushed out of his chair and strolled over to the window—windows being a vulnerable spot for bullets should one of the many people who wanted Mark dead track him down.

No one bothered him more than Rudolph Manzinni, a man so meticulous, neither Mark nor Luciano had ever met him. So very few people in the syndicate had. A man whose reputation for revenge kept even the most ruthless syndicate members in line. What would Rudolph do if Mark failed again?

The man's resources seemed endless. He'd hunted down escaped members to far-flung places across the globe. Just as Mark had hoped the Stonewall deal would grant him freedom, or at least significant distance, the entire operation folded, and he was left to feel damn lucky just to be alive.

Much of his assets had been seized. All he had left was a cache of physical cash he'd kept hidden from everyone. And now he needed to be more careful than ever.

His next plans had to unfold flawlessly. Before the law or anyone else could stop him. So, first priority was to stay hidden. To not get caught. With that in mind, he stepped away from the window's light and the tranquil view of a wide front yard, complete with thick greenery and floral garden arch.

He'd return to his task of gathering help from his syndicate contacts, to picking up the phone and making more calls. Perhaps Rudolph being pissed wasn't such a bad thing. Mark now had the entire syndicate working toward his success. He had room for one big and final plan. To fulfill his promise to level all of Harlow into extinction.

He would make an example out of that God-awful town. Would show the world what came of anyone who crossed him. Sure enough, he'd turn the people of Harlow into prisoners in their own homes— and just like prisoners—they would dream of escape where none existed.

Maybe everyone figured him to be down and out, but truth was, he had even more ambition than before. He would watch from afar as, one by one, each resident reached their breaking point and turned on the others. Not such a sweet little town after all. He'd make each resident into a hypocrite. Show them that they weren't all that different to him.

Now, all that remained was to decide how much he would give up getting all that he wanted.

Six

THREE DAYS after Emilia's wedding and Laila stood at the black iron gates of Harlow Municipal Gardens, her fingers curled around the handlebar of Whitney's abandoned hot-pink scooter. The little girl skipped ahead and chatted to the yellow daisies along the gravel path, all the while heading toward the bright orange swings in the playground up ahead.

Laila's explanation to Whitney about today was that they were here to meet and get to know their new neighbor, Ramos, who was definitely just a potential "friend." As much as Whitney had gleefully accepted that version of the truth, she'd asked endless questions about Ramos, wanting to know what shows he liked or whether he liked the same food as her. Of course, Laila couldn't answer any of that. She barely knew the man. Which only left her running her gaze over these pristine gardens and the too-perfect blue sky, while wondering why she'd ever expressed an interest in meeting up today.

Seeing Chip and Ally back together and so happy had made spontaneous emotion drown out her better sense. Or maybe it was the ache that came with remembering just how many years had passed since she'd had a similar private life.

Her stomach churned and she felt overly hot. The last date she'd been on was some five years ago and long before Whitney's birth. Now, the heaviness of guilt only sank deeper into her tummy, because even this playground setting made this rendezvous feel like not a date at all. As though the chances were strong that her complex situation would prove too much for Ramos and he'd make some excuse to bail.

Who am I kidding?

That said, him seeing the reality of dating a single mom wasn't such a bad thing. Both her parents worked. As did she. It was near impossible to get an evening off for any kind of socializing. So, daytime park dates it had to be. Perhaps she could just relax now and let "real life" take care of this man.

And speaking of the man, Ramos rose from a gray metal bench farther up the path, then embarked on a far-too-casual stroll her way. Her heartbeat climbed with his every step. He wore what she'd already decided was his uniform of black t-shirt, dark jeans, and a self-satisfied smile. But before he could reach her, Whitney got to him first.

"Hey, Mister Man!" Whitney yelled the over exuberant welcome and swung her arm up in the air, directing a decisive high-five his way.

In the next beat, she was gone, off to claim the one free seat on the swings. The corners of his eyes crinkled from his genuine grin, and he stalked closer to Laila, while she pressed a knuckle to her mouth and fought to restrain her laughter. Thanks, Whitney. What an ice breaker.

A portion of calm took over and she decided to help close the distance toward him, soon extending her arms in what felt like a date-appropriate hug.

She drew back and tried to ignore the spicy-earth scent coming off his skin, nudging her head Whitney's way. "Sorry 'bout that, and sorry we're a bit late. Leaving the house with a kid, not easy, yah know?"

He gave a relaxed shrug. "All good. I would have offered to walk down with you, but I didn't want to assume. I'm just glad you made it."

Despite the light dance of his gaze over her face and the soft smile on his lips, his comment suggested he'd half expected her not to show. Not that she could blame his skepticism.

"Yah well, good assumption." She nodded to the playground, hinting that they should walk on. "I drove anyway, there's no knowing when Whit will get tired, and her legs will suddenly refuse to work. There are bags of cement lighter than a toddler who doesn't want to walk."

Though she cringed at already shifting the conversation to her child, he gave nothing but an encouraging chuckle. "I bought us coffee from Main Street. Seems you might need it. They might even still be warm."

He tilted his head to the bench he'd been seated on, two paper coffee cups indeed waiting here. Despite not needing caffeine to prod extra life into her already racing heart, she gave a grateful groan all the same. "You're a saint."

He reached out and took over the duty of dragging Whitney's scooter along, meanwhile, Laila drew a breath and absorbed the sweet, mid-summer Minnesotan air. "I can't remember the last time I did something like this."

"You mean, went on a date?" He turned and raised a brow her way, and she gave a small laugh.

"Well, yeah, that, but I also mean just getting out of the house to meet other actual adults."

"Didn't I just see you at a wedding?"

She laughed again and swatted gently at his bicep with the back of her hand. "As fun as that was, weddings don't count. I kinda have to show up to those."

"Whereas this was a choice?" His smile grew, revealing that he knew he had her and she'd inadvertently admitted too much.

He quietly parked the scooter near the bench and collected the two coffees, handing one to her.

"All I mean is, I feel like my life revolves around dropping Whit off at her grandparents, then racing away to work or study." She eyed her coffee cup's black plastic lid and ignored the obvious dip to her voice. "It's just nice to have a change of routine."

Even if this is very likely temporary.

"Yeah, I get that." Even if she didn't look up at him, his deep tone made the understanding in his statement sound genuine. "Though it seems Whitney is lucky to have you."

Her body turned rigid, and she instinctively jerked her chin up, a confusing fluttery feeling taking hold beneath her ribcage. "It never feels like that. It always feels like she never has my full attention, and that she'll wake up one day and lay into me over all the ways I've failed her."

He narrowed his eyes at her in a thoughtful look and shook his head, soon turning his focus to Whitney who currently ran between playground equipment with two older kids. Even just that small gesture gave Laila the rare sensation that, for this one short moment, she wasn't carrying the sole burden of watching over her child.

"She won't remember it like that."

Once again, the steady certainty in his words left her gaping at him, while the muscles over her chest locked up in inexplicable defense. His certainty left the impression he knew something she didn't. "How would you know what she'll remember?"

His gaze flicked to her, but only for a second, before he went back to watching ahead. "I'm the kid of a single mom too. I have a little experience on my side here."

A neutral silence lingered now, and still, his gaze didn't meet hers —almost as though he didn't want to look at her—perhaps because he'd revealed something of himself. Or maybe because he'd managed to best her once again. So, she buried her thoughts by taking her first sip of coffee, and then mumbling a few limp words over the rim. "I guess that figures."

Is this just a pity date? Or does experience make him a little more understanding than most?

"I remember my mom being forever busy as well." Again, his focus stayed forward, as if he still wasn't ready to face her, though his husky tone expressed more than any look could. "But I also remember feeling really lucky. Unlike my dad, she stuck around."

He turned to Laila and shrugged, his brow creased at the center and heavy. "She was my lifeline, Laila. Yes, her inability to be everywhere all at once frustrated me at times, but life and maturity sorted those memories out soon enough. More than anything, I look back and just admire her. She could have given up, but she never did."

Once more, silence swallowed the exchange, but for a whole other reason than awkwardness. His words stirred something within her, something she'd never really acknowledged as being important, and so she found herself blinking up and seeing him with an entirely new light.

What happened to the overly smooth bonehead I thought I'd be meeting with today?

She gave a lighthearted scoff of laughter and dredged her ability to splutter out a reply. "Wow. You might have just given me a glimpse down the end of the long and dark parenting tunnel."

He offered another laugh, one that gathered the golden skin over his cheekbones, even as he took a drink of coffee and offered her his side-long stare. Yet another rare moment passed here. One where she actually did believe him. Where she felt like maybe she was doing an okay job. Even though she had no shortage of her own family saying so.

Hearing those words from someone still so new to her—a child of a single parent at that—she pulled her attention away from him because the swelling sensation in her chest threatened to overwhelm.

Next, she cleared her throat and set to reprise a casual air. "I'm assuming your mother is still with us?"

"Still in LA and living it up with her friends." One corner of his lip rose with a bashful looking smirk. "Though not too busy to call most days just to chew me out over when I'm gonna make her an abuela."

From her few spare moments watching the movie *Encanto* with Whitney, Laila recognized that the word "abuela" meant "grandmother" and joined him in laughing.

That said, this *was* a date, and she already had a child, while he'd just indicated a need for some biological children of his own. So, she raised a brow and mumbled over the rim of her coffee cup. "No pressure, or anything..."

He patted her between the shoulder blades and chuckled, his light touch sending unexpected sparks through her body. "Relax. I have a younger brother and he's already got two kids. I'm mostly off the hook. My mom's just never happy, that's all."

He swung a big smile her way, one that suggested sarcasm about his mom's unhappiness. While appreciating being "off the hook," his smile prompted her next genuine laugh.

An easy silence took over and they both turned to Whitney, now attempting to run up the wrong end of a slide, as the two other kids waited way-too-patiently for her to move out the way.

Laila and Ramos shared a joint quiet chuckle before he spoke again. "At the wedding, you mentioned Whitney's dad isn't around?"

The fluttery light feeling in her tummy evaporated, replaced with something far heavier, which made forming a reply take longer than she would have liked. "Yah. I did."

More silence dragged out. She figured he wanted her to elaborate, but even after four years, shame and heartache still consumed her every time anyone asked for a recap of her and Whitney's story.

Much to her despair, Ramos seemed to grasp the weight of her stalling, his torso twisting in her direction, as he eyeballed her from side-on. "Mind me asking what happened?"

Yes. She *did* mind. But then his tone held a soft edge that offered her a way out if she didn't wish to explain—the annoying thing about that being his steady presence and his "way out" succeeded in compelling her to answer all the same.

Seven

"MIKE. Whitney's dad's name is Mike, and all I know, all I can really say about him is that he simply disappeared." Laila shrugged as if that empty account of things didn't hurt. Truth was, she really did have no other explanation.

Adrian's twisted and confused features had her fusing her attention away from him, back to the playground where Whitney still played. "Whitney was a surprise and the result of a completely unplanned pregnancy. Mike and I, we'd been together for two years, which I guess is forever when you're young and in a town like Harlow. Yah know, by most people's standards here, we should've been married with three kids already—"

She gave a sarcastic laugh, and he shuffled beside her, sipping at his coffee cup and resuming his air of being unstirred. "If you'd been together two years, the math on three kids doesn't quite add up on that one."

She gave a light huff and added, "Not if I managed to squeeze in a set of twins, but either way, welcome to small town life. As you can imagine, we were both shocked when we found out about Whitney, but we seemed to adjust well enough early on—right down to the quickie wedding and a pinky promise that we would get through this

SMALL TOWN SECRETS   39

together. But things changed just after Whitney was born, and Mike got laid off from his job as a factory hand at a food processing warehouse one town over.

"She couldn't have been much more than three months old before we were at the edge of bankruptcy, with no way to pay the rent and bills. That's when Mike started referring to Whit and me as 'dead weight,' that we were holding him back, and he didn't have time to deal with us while trying to find a job."

"He sounds like a real charmer." Adrian shook his head and turned to face her. "Did this guy ever have any redeeming qualities?"

"Only if you're a naïve young woman with not much life experience. A woman who hasn't learned how to ask for any of her needs to be met." She sighed, and decided to go ahead with her story, despite this not being her ideal topic. "Like I said, Mike changed a lot. Like the life had been sucked right out of him or something. Nothing made much sense, except that Whitney was relying on me. So, less than a few months after giving birth to her, I took things into my own hands and asked for my old job back at the twenty-four-hour grocery store. Deep down I didn't trust Mike to take care of Whit on his own, so I arranged for my parents to look after her while I worked. For better or worse, Mike hung on for a couple more months before up and leaving. No goodbye. No letter. No explanation. Just me returning from work one day to an empty home."

"That's not exactly a scene anyone wants to walk into."

A lump took up space in her throat, and she peered down and nodded at the coffee cup in her hand. "No shit. At first, I feared the worst and was frantic trying to find him. Had he died? Harlow being so remote, maybe his car ran off some road somewhere and no one would ever find his body. Except, five days in, a stack of money disappeared from our joint bank account, and he blocked me from all his social media profiles. And just like that, a few weeks passed before the divorce papers came from some out-of-town lawyer."

Another laugh pushed past her lips at just how ridiculous the story sounded out loud. Growing up, she'd had the perfect family. The perfect life. But she and the relationship with Mike had been central to all that was wrong with her life now. An unplanned pregnancy. Young love gone wrong. A runaway ex...

"Mike refused to speak with me. I didn't have the head space or the money to drag things out, and to this day, he still fails to make payments on Whit's child support. So, I take care of everything. And still, I question whether our troubles were all Mike, or all me. I still don't know what I did to make him hate me so much."

She'd had dreams. Always assumed she'd have years to find her way and get settled in life before slowing down to have a child. She'd always assumed she'd be financially secure first, that there'd be room for her to stay at home at least for those early years.

But babies needed to eat first and foremost. They needed shelter and warmth. So those basic needs came before any of her dreams, in the hopes that the rest would come when she'd paid her penance for those past mistakes.

"Here I am, four years on." She pressed her lips together and gave Ramos an *Oh, well* sort of shrug. "Still working in that grocery store and hoping my degree will dig us out of that pit."

Adrian's face held a tight kind of stillness and he side-eyed her. "Did you ever find out where Mike went?"

She dropped her gaze to his hands clenched around his coffee cup, the white strain over his knuckles giving her the laughable thought that he might sucker punch Mike if he just happened to be around right now.

"Beyond some initial searching"—she shook her head—"save for the hassle of not getting child support, I'm glad to have him gone. Given the way he was, I'm going to go right ahead and assume he's still miserable, unemployed, and probably forever single or hopping from one bad relationship to the next. If there's one thing I want Whit to understand about love, it's that she should never have to convince anyone to stick around or pull their weight. Her dad included."

Adrian's stare shifted ahead, his brow flexed in a hard line, a strong current of emotion evident in his eyes. So much so, she took a deep breath and sought to ease the tension. "Look, I'm sorry, I gave you a hard time over getting me to agree to this date. At least maybe now you understand why."

"Right. And what I'm up against should I choose to proceed?" His stare narrowed some more, before he angled his attention back to her and the strain across his face released into a sly smile. "It's okay, I enjoy a challenge."

"Well, good luck with that." She barked out a sarcastic laugh. "Though I guess it probably is time I learned to let my guard down more."

He made a clicking sound with one corner of his mouth and shook his head. "Nah, that's not it. I've worked enough investigation jobs to have seen a thing or two. Cheating husbands and much worse. Too many women are raised to be welcoming at all costs, but if I had a daughter, you better believe my advice would be that any guards she might have up are built on experience and intuition. That any defensive urges are most often right, and it's easier to ask forgiveness than permission, so you might as well put your needs and safety first. At least in the beginning, anyway."

She raised a brow and put on a flat tone, even though his words melted a certain kind of hardness she hadn't before noticed around her heart. "So, I shouldn't be on this date with you?"

"Sure, you should, but I get that you have no reason to trust me. Just like you said, you shouldn't have to persuade someone to love you. The same could apply to trust. Doubly so when you've got a kid to protect." He jutted his chin to Whitney but held a clear levity in his expression. "The way I see it, trust comes from consistent good behavior. That means from both parties. I'm still sussing you out too, you know. Though count this conversation as your reminder to stop straight-up assuming it's always you who's the problem."

He pressed his lips into a matter-of-fact line and shrugged, her pulse shifting from a thundering beat to a slow plod, her mouth parting while she worked through this man's astute theories on relationships and women. Given that she was a woman he wanted to pursue, his honest opinion over manipulation was especially unexpected.

Don't get ahead of yourself. This might all be part of his plan...

Still stunned, she grasped for something to say, or even just a firmer hold over her thoughts on this man, only for salvation to come in the form of Maureen Cooper charging across the gardens toward her.

"Maureen?" Laila's question lashed free of her, though not wholly unjustified given Maureen's flushed face. "Everything alright?"

"Yes, yes everything's fine." Maureen came to a stop, her breaths a fast pant and her gaze bouncing between Laila and Ramos, before her small scowl eased into a light smile. Already this woman reached her own conclusions about why these two stood here sipping coffee together. "I just came from a meeting with the out-of-town lawyer who stops by to offer legal advice at the council from time to time."

Not wanting to think the worst, Laila suppressed a frown. "Lawyer?"

"Yah bet." Maureen's eyes lit with a thankfully excited gleam, which probably meant she wasn't looking to divorce Frank or sue someone. "The General Store received a buy-out offer, so I'm doing some due-diligence before we make any decisions."

"Wait! What?" Laila pressed a hand to her chest, her attention for some reason flicking to Ramos in search of support, before even that disconcerting action had her turning back to Maureen. "Buy-out? Maureen, you're thinking of selling?"

Harlow's one and only General Store had been a core part of this community since long before Laila's birth, and right now, she couldn't begin to imagine the place belonging to anyone other than the Coopers.

"Oh, I don't know." Maureen swatted a hand in a gesture both dramatic and dismissive. "We had no plans on selling, but then the amount of money on offer... Let's just say, we'd be featherbrained not to at least entertain the idea."

"Hang on a minute." Adrian narrowed his stare on Maureen, the action slow like a prowling cat homing in on prey. "Is the offer from someone local?"

Maureen shrugged and shook her head. "People 'round here don't tend to have that sort of money. All I know is it's from an LLC called Forrex Co. My guess is it's no local. Even the lawyer just now seemed unable to offer much help on identifying our buyer."

"Do me a favor"—Adrian held a momentary pause, which only

highlighted the gentle warning in his lowered tone—"Don't make any decisions until I look into this for you. It won't take long. Can you do that for me?"

Maureen shrugged again, her face soon lighting up. "Sure thing, that'd be much appreciated. Yah know, despite the money, Frank and I don't want to sell to just anyone."

Though Maureen's promise offered some relief, Laila's stomach still churned. The general store sustained so many people in this town and anyone buying the place would hold the power to affect a lot of lives.

That said, Adrian's questions concerned Laila too. Those questions came as a reminder of why he was in town. To protect everyone. To put himself between this town and the syndicate. And as much as being around him already offered her warm and easy feelings, this reminder woke her to the fact that not all was *easy* with this man.

He had a past, and his present was also seeped in danger. Then again, so was hers. Which only deepened the unsettling feeling that she would have to trust this man—this relative stranger—in more ways than she'd ever wanted to trust a man again.

Eight

THE SKY HAD DARKENED by the time Adrian sat in the passenger seat of Laila's car, now parked in her driveway. He'd accepted her offer for a lift home and Whitney slept in the backseat, tuckered out from her playground adventure, followed with a stroll down Main Street for food and then ice cream. So, Ramos savored the silence and willed this date to linger a little longer. Even though Laila's story about her ex gripped him with an oppressive kind of restlessness.

Despite all these years and his own absent father, he still couldn't understand how someone could be so cold toward the mother of their child. *Much less the child themselves.* A part of him itched to unleash his skills and track down Mike. To figure out what his deal was and give the man a piece of his mind. An irrational overstep, sure, but he took some of what he'd learned today personally. That said, he had too much respect for Laila to find this man without her consent.

He turned to his right and caught her gaze, her inky blue stare dark against the night and sweeping about his face. Though his heart pounded in response, he held still, aware that the arrival home was where many dates ended with a kiss.

But her situation was more complicated than any woman he'd dated, and her child *did* still sleep just behind him.

"I should get Whitney inside." Though she leveled a half-smile his way, her voice had fallen to a soft whisper and the edges of her eyes smoothed in a way that shifted something inside him. As if she didn't want to wake Whitney. Or dare he hope that she wanted this date to continue?

But he didn't know the general ground rules of dating a single mother. Didn't want to rush things or intimidate this woman, especially since he still had to live next to her. So, he gave a decisive nod and pushed his door open, set to helping her and Whitney get inside their house.

The evening held the moon's silver-blue tinge as he stepped outside and turned for Whitney's door, assuming the task of some moderate lifting and carrying the child out.

Except, he didn't make it too far before bumping into Laila powering toward the same door. He caught her forearms in time to save her from stumbling.

"Jeez Louise!" Her hand came to rest on his chest, as she steadied her footing; before she gave a shaky laugh and snatched her hand back. "I'm so sorry."

Jeez Louise? He chuckled at the Minnesotan turn of phrase, only for his heart to do a hard thud against his chest wall. Her jovial stare fused to his, falling into complete seriousness, her face slack, while wide pools of black drowned the bright blue in her eyes.

She caught the moment too. The prickling energy urging them together. Perhaps she wanted the typical date ending, after all, but again, he refused to assume.

That said, he wasn't any kind of saint and still wanted what he wanted, which in this case was *her*. So, he leaned in, providing a clue that she need only say yes.

"Please. No."

Not the answer he hoped for!

And even as her hands lashed out and grabbed his wrists, he did as commanded and shifted ever so slightly back.

New panic entered her eyes, her stare darting side-to-side and over his face. "I'm so sorry… It's just…"

His thoughts slipped back to their earlier talk about not having to work so hard for affection. The time had come to take his own advice.

"It's fine." He moved to step back, but her fingers curled harder into the flesh of his arms. "Some other time, maybe."

She gave her head a wild shake and tugged him closer. "It's just been a while, yah know? Years, even. And I... I..."

Her voice continued to trail and then she pressed her lips into a resigned, hard line, but he caught her meaning—that this was hugely unfamiliar territory—that nerves got the better of her and she didn't know what to do next.

His shoulders eased and new air filled his lungs, as he dared to seek a direct answer. "So, you want me to?"

He leaned in again, this time lifting a hand to her cheek and making his own intentions clear. She drew in too and nodded, her fingers releasing from his wrists and rising toward his face, only to fumble around his already raised arms.

Color rose in her cheeks, and he bit back a chuckle, not wanting to embarrass her, while far more invested in helping her navigate unfamiliar territory. He caught her hands and placed them to his chest, the speed of her breaths quickening, though his own racing heartbeat laughed at his ideas that he was the one in control here. "It's okay. It's just a kiss."

The words seemed to hang for a long moment, and he couldn't be sure which one of them needed more support or convincing. Still, her wide stare held, and she gave a shaky nod.

"It's okay." He whispered the words and pulled her closer, cradling her face in his hands. Though he drew his lips closer, her eyes remained open, and she failed to breathe. "It's okay."

He made his voice softer still and her muscles relaxed beneath his hold. "It's okay."

Softer and softer he spoke those words, until her eyelids drifted shut and she tilted her chin up to him. He shuttered his eyes too, and in the next beat, his world went dark, and the heat of her lips met his. Her pillowy skin there had him holding back a low groan. As much as he wanted to slow this down and give her a full experience, he also gave himself the gift of pressing her into him and driving the kiss deeper.

She released a weak murmur and went evermore pliable in his arms. If not for the sleeping kid in the car, he would have pressed Laila against the cold, hard metal and ravaged her in any and every way she would let him.

He wasn't used to leashing his desire, and right about now, every exploding and hot sensation within him screamed for release. He wanted to run his hands lower. To explore her body in ways most other women he dated didn't seem to mind. But this wasn't his usual date. And Laila wasn't his usual woman. If he pushed her too far, chances were she'd run.

But even as he contemplated giving her some space, her delicate taste and touch enveloped him, and her fingers curled into his chest. Her own need rose in her soft sighs and the heat from her body exuded the restraint-snapping scent of her fruit and musk perfume.

Just as he thought this moment might be his undoing, she released a frustrated groan and broke the kiss, her forehead coming to rest on his, while her shoulders rose and fell with a series of bursting breaths.

Her hazy stare rose to meet his in a look he could only describe as lost wonder and apology. "Thank you."

He startled at her gratitude but steered away from voicing his surprise. Never had a woman thanked him for kissing her, but then, he'd never been on a date with a woman and her kid, much less helped that woman overcome a personal hurdle by kissing her. So, her gratitude made at least a little sense.

Since his stay in town would be short-lived and the life he'd carved out came with no real plans, he frowned at the strong likelihood of his "help" one day benefitting some other man.

He didn't want to dwell on that thought and so turned for Whitney's door, only for Laila's hand to catch him before he could pull at the handle.

"Let me do this one, okay?" Her lips curled into a soft smile and her brows pressed closer in that look of easy gratitude again.

So stirring. So unsettling. Yet he stepped back and honored her wishes, having already gotten the strong impression this woman was used to doing most things on her own.

Besides, him carrying Whitney would mean going into Laila's house, and Laila had every right and reason not to want that. Not yet anyway.

She leaned into the car and pulled Whitney from her seat, the little girl's head lolling forward onto her mother's shoulder without a care in the world. He stayed close enough to help close the car door, then stood in the driveway to watch Laila heft her daughter onto her front porch and into her house, but not before freeing a hand from Whitney and sending him a quick smile and wave goodbye.

The sweet parting left him with nothing to do but stroll around the short picket fence between the two houses and up his own driveway, all while lugging the weight of what had just happened. *The potential. The risk.*

He hadn't thought much about his expectations with Laila. Not beyond getting her to agree to this date. Only now, an unfamiliar strain gripped at his heart and hinted at something much bigger than what his peas-sized brain had bargained on.

Something fragile. Something complicated. Something riddled with warnings. Warnings he most definitely would ignore and live to regret.

Just like any person, he didn't know what the future had in store. In fact, *more* than most, he'd never really cared to find out. Except for now, when a swimming sensation took over his head and his heart, anticipation sweeping hot electricity over his skin and spurring his hurried steps to his front door.

"Hey!"

He paused at Laila's loud greeting, taking a moment before looking at her. As bright as her tone sounded, there came that warning again…

When he did look, she stood on her landing, arm waving high above her head, her weight lifted onto her toes, as she craned her neck in a bid for his full attention. He wanted to smile at that, to level a smile as carefree as hers, but the prickling at his skin continued.

Don't fall too fast.

Still, he wouldn't block her out completely, and rather than round the two driveways, he ambled closer to the fence between them and waited for her to join him. "What is it?"

She jogged toward him and paused a beat, grinning up at him, before she grabbed the front of his shirt and pulled him in. He had no time to gather his senses, before she had him snared in another kiss, one she controlled completely.

Her lips held a hungry force, and her hands held firm to the sides of his face, as if she'd had a moment to think about their last kiss and returned to tie up unfinished business.

Just as quickly as things had started, she released him on a joyful smile. Her stunning blue eyes glittered up at him, while he remained stunned, but pleasantly so.

His astonishment broke only as she turned tail and jogged back to her door, where she punched a hand into the air at her landing and released an excited squeal. All-too-soon, she disappeared back into her house.

Nine

THAT SAME NIGHT, the smell of wood and alcohol greeted Rochelle as she crossed the floor at Maynard's and took a seat at the bar.

"Back again?" Sarah strode over, her amber-green eyes sparkling with a bemused sort of joy. She looked from Rochelle to the kitchen pass where Gordon worked, then back to Rochelle. "I'd offer to let you lodge in our wine cellar, but I hear Gordon's already moved you into his place."

Rochelle's mouth dropped open while she struggled a beat. Although Sarah had a point, Richelle *had* stopped by Maynard's most of the five nights she'd lingered in Harlow, she was yet to get her head around how straight-to-the-point most people in these parts were.

I thought I was the only brutally honest one.

"I wouldn't go that far." Just as she mumbled that reply, a blonde woman in her twenties gave a little *squeak* to her right.

"You and Gordon are dating? Gordon has a girlfriend?" The blonde's voice pitched upward at the end, and she bounced in her seat, repeatedly patting the arm of a man beside her in a gesture for him to participate in the conversation.

Once again, Rochelle sat dumbfounded. Once again, she wanted to utter the same reply, "*I wouldn't go that far.*" But her weekend in

Harlow had evolved into nearly a week of living with a man she'd met off-the-cuff, and so far, she still struggled to leave.

It was way too early in the relationship to even try to define who she was to him or tackle the challenge of living literal states apart if they did want to keep seeing each other. Perhaps not wanting to address any of that confusion came from denial. In truth, she didn't really know what she was doing, only that she didn't want this current escapade to end.

"Oh, gosh! I'm being rude." The woman pressed one hand to her cheek and stuck the other out for Rochelle to shake. "I'm sorry. I'm Ally Egan, and this man beside me is Chip. My boyfriend. I'm moving into his house too. Isn't that exciting?"

"Pleasure to meet you." Rochelle accepted the handshake but flattened her voice into a dry but light tone, refusing to touch the topic of her "moving in" with Gordon. "That's *not* what's happening with Gordon and me."

Ally's smile stilled, and her gaze dropped to the bar's counter. After a while, she released a deflated, "Oh..." Her gaze bounced back up and her eyes lighted again before her voice took on a stronger, "Oooooohhhhh!"

Not wanting to elaborate, mostly because there wasn't much to share, Rochelle turned to Sarah. "Give me anything with gin in it."

Sarah chuckled, seeming to catch Rochelle's need for a breather, and went about expertly assembling that drink. She plucked a bottle of gin off the shelf behind her and poured a measure into a glass, followed by tonic water, ice, and a squeeze of lime juice. With a practiced flourish of her wrist, she finished with an edible flower floating on top.

"On the house." She winked and nodded to Ally. "Ally is a lot to handle, but she means well, and we're not all so inquisitive."

"Hey!" Even through Ally's protest, Chip chuckled into the back of his hand, his hazel gaze connecting with Rochelle.

"Either way, it's nice to meet you." He flicked a thumb to an older couple on his opposite side. "These are her parents, Vel and Ronny, so mind what you say."

Rochelle let out a laugh and, thankfully, so did Ally's parents. Ally, on the other hand, held a slightly offended frown, though the small wobble of her lips said she didn't wholly object to the summary of her character.

Vel extended a warm and gentle look, and spoke next. "Ally is our youngest daughter, we have another, Laila. That one's a smidge more restrained, but I hope you can understand Al's curiosity. Gordon has always been mysterious about his private life, yah know. It's a nice surprise to see him with someone."

Rochelle clicked her tongue against the roof of her mouth. "Sure, I get it, but I've known the guy for less than a week, and we're certainly not in any sort of relationship." She could feel the weight of everyone listening, so she added with more enthusiasm. "What I can say is, it's been an adventure so far."

Hoping her upbeat reply might score Gordon some social points long after she returned to LA, but aware more questions might be incoming, she took a quick sip of her drink and veered her gaze.

Maybe she should have called her time here a "reverse adventure." Her life had slowed all the way down, and Gordon was the unassuming sort, who gave the impression he spent much of his life being largely underestimated. That probably explained why she'd been able to invade his kitchen that first night, only to invite herself into his life outright.

But she liked that about him.

Unlike so many other men she encountered, he didn't seem to take her brash approach personally or try to compete. He kind of just rolled with the punches. He was a still lake to her squally ocean. A man capable of being around just the right amount that she needed.

He left her to her solo morning walks in the majestic woods out the back of his house. Sometimes he'd have breakfast cooked on her return. Sometimes they would do that bit together. He gave her space to handle her current workload online, with afternoons and evenings outside of his work hours spent together. They'd settled into a routine so fast, but so non-dramatic. Like she'd been given her first moment in years to stop and breathe.

And then there was this town, with her visits to the local attractions, including the nursery, where a boisterous elderly woman by the name of Aggie McKey swept her up in a wild conversation Rochelle hadn't exactly invited, but had come to enjoy either way. She'd learned a bit of town history and how Aggie's family had lived in these parts for generations. How she'd married her childhood sweetheart and been devoted to him ever since, even though he'd passed away some twenty years ago.

Rochelle couldn't imagine a love like that, but still she found herself absorbed in the romanticism of Aggie's story. Rochelle's life in LA just seemed to move too fast. As much as she loved her family and friends, everyone was always so busy, while everyone here—especially Gordon —seemed to have nothing *but* time.

And perhaps that's why she failed to leave.

She peered up and watched Gordon through the pass, his red flannel shirtsleeves extending out from his pale blue apron, his broad back mostly to her and his head tilted down. He handled multiple pans on the stove in a skilled, calm rhythm.

Her heart jolted at the sight of him, at the effect he and these unobtrusive surroundings had on her. Again, she sipped at her citrusy astringent drink in search of diversion, her thoughts sticking on the empty feeling that had slowly crept into her life in recent years.

That feeling had taken up space in her heart and stolen joy from things that once brought her delight. Amidst achieving all her goals and chasing every thrill. Amidst the years of exploring exciting places and cultures, her jet-set life left her void of one major thing. *Connection.*

But everyone she encountered in Harlow provided that in spades. From the festivities at Emilia's wedding, to this scene at the bar, everyone welcomed her. No wonder Emilia had changed her initial plans to run from Harlow only to stay.

"Say, Ally, why don't you invite Rochelle to your house-warming party?" Sarah gave a sly smile and leaned into the bar, making it clear she was invested in giving Rochelle more reasons to stick around.

"Oh, that's a great idea." Ally clapped her hands together and sent Rochelle an expectant look, one that left Rochelle feeling uncharacteristically uncertain.

She turned to Sarah and gave her a light-hearted glare before addressing Ally. "When is it?"

Ally lashed out her hands and clung onto Rochelle's forearm as though she'd already said *yes*. "In two days. It's nothing big, yah know, since the house was Chip's childhood home, and he was already living there. I just want to celebrate us being back together and me moving in." She clamped her lips together as if she knew she was kind of rambling, only to speak again. "There'll be just a few of us, but as long as you're with Gordon, you're one of us. Your invite is a given."

Two days?

One of them?

She'd been taking each day in Harlow as it came with no real plans on what she'd do next, but *now* she had plans. In two days. And it seemed her connection with Gordon made her an honorary Harlow resident.

Her heart strained from the added pressure and confusion. Things with Gordon were still so new, so much so it felt weird even calling whatever they had a relationship. At the same time, the tightness in her chest loosened to a quick flutter because Ally's invite offered an unfamiliar sense of belonging. A small corner for Rochelle's heart longed to find out what sticking around would do for her as a person and her relationship with Gordon.

Once again, she was being pulled in, but in all her years of extravagant adventures, her last five days somehow still ranked amongst petting elephants in Laos and lounging on yachts by sun-kissed Greek Islands. Harlow was just... a different kind of fun. Far more humble and easygoing. She had money and a thriving business, but she'd never truly settled anywhere for very long. Maybe Harlow had something new to teach her. Maybe she could afford to *stop*. To experience what it meant to belong somewhere.

So, she turned to Ally and offered a definite smile. "That is a very kind offer. I'll see you in two days."

An exquisite wide grin crept across Ally's face, and Rochelle turned to watch Gordon through the pass, the man remaining steady through the chaos of Maynard's kitchen and a multitude of orders. Even if her time in Harlow had started as a simple weekend away, she'd always been a fan of change, and right now, she vowed to make her stay here something so much more.

She would see this place through different eyes. Through the eyes of someone more like her friend, Emilia. She'd come from the same city and social group as Rochelle, only to become blissfully immersed with everything to do with Harlow. And maybe Rochelle could do that too. Maybe she could slow down and find a minute to fully explore small-town life and fall in love.

Ten

THE NEXT EVENING, Maynard's Tavern neared closing time and only a few patrons remained for last drinks, the general hubbub of the venue having long died down. Adrian sat surrounded by six familiar faces at a round table in a corner of the room, the quiet and quaint surroundings doing nothing to dull their expressions of anger, fear, and concern.

Since he'd been the one to call this meeting, Ramos was the first to speak, turning his stiff gaze to Maureen and Frank Cooper. "I've looked into the LLC wanting to buy your store and the news isn't good. There's not much information on them, in fact, it's been actively suppressed. They don't show any history of ever being in the food supply industry, which seems suspicious for a company looking to buy a small-town grocery store. I don't see what they stand to gain from obtaining the store."

Dean leaned his weight forward and into the table, his unaffected tone cutting in. "Especially if they're offering more cash than required."

The sheriff nodded and turned to Maureen. "I hate to say it, but this does seem too good to be true."

"You think it's the syndicate?" Maureen's face turned pale, and she pulled her wide stare from the sheriff and onto her husband, a series of worried glances breaking out between everyone in attendance—Sarah and Gordon included.

"We don't need any more convincing." Frank directed his decisive words to his wife, his forehead scored in a crosshatch of vexed wrinkles. "We'll decline their offer first thing in the morning."

The strain across Maureen's face eased a little and she gave a slow nod, before peering around at the others at the table. "I guess that settles it then. This whole ordeal has been so overwhelming, but I'm thankful for everyone's help."

"Still kinda worrying, dontcha think?" Sarah frowned at Adrian, her fingers curled into the black apron she'd pulled from around her waist before sitting down, that apron now a bundled heap on the table. "That the syndicate might be vying to buy up local businesses?"

Just as he was about to answer, he sensed someone standing behind him and an unfamiliar feminine voice cut in. "Hey!"

He twisted just as a woman in her late twenties leaned over to hug Gordon seated to his left. With her designer clothes and meticulously styled appearance, she seemed out of character from most others in this town.

Gordon leaped from his chair and put his arm around the woman's waist, his proud grin directed at his friends. "Not sure if everyone's met Rochelle yet, but she's Emilia's friend from LA and she stopped by for the wedding."

"She's met a whole lot of your friends already, Gordon. Heck, she even scored an invite to Ally's housewarming." Sarah pitched one eyebrow higher at Gordon and leveled a bored tone, though the wide smile on her lips said she was happy for him. "It's clear she's stayed for more than the wedding."

"What can I say?" He swept a hand down over himself. "Harlow has a lot to offer."

Rochelle chuckled and shook her head, her gaze skimming over the small gathering. "And still, there are a few unfamiliar faces here now. Nice to meet everyone." She waved at the table at large, then turned and peered up at Gordon. "Have I interrupted something? Do you need more time? I can wait."

"We were just discussing town security." The sheriff interjected this time, even as he moved to stand. "And we were just finishing up, but I hear you were one of the people caught up in the B&B closure when you first arrived."

"I was." Rochelle's small frown only lasted as long as it took her to peer back at Gordon. "Not that I'm still pissed about that. Getting locked out led me to meeting this one."

She nodded to Gordon, then returned her attention to the sheriff, something Ramos also did, as he spoke again. "The B&B is closed?"

The sheriff stared back for a quiet and heavy beat, his expression hardening with each passing second. "Sold off and closed, yah. What with the Coopers' recent experience, do you think we have the early stages of a pattern here?"

Not wanting to admit to much, Ramos held back from answering right away. "Disrupting business would be a good way to get revenge without having to set foot in this town."

"Mark Farro was bad enough." Dean's attention bounced from one person to the next, his hands curled into fists atop the table. "With Rudolph Manzinni said to be involved, anything's possible."

Again, Adrian didn't want to say much, didn't want to scare the people at this table more than they already were, certainly didn't want to add more conjecture to the panic and rumors buzzing around this town. So, he peered up at Rochelle and puzzled over her suddenly washed-out complexion and slack cheeks, as though the mention of Rudolph Manzinni's name bothered her even more than the people genuinely tied to this town.

"Mark's still on the run though, right?" Though Sarah spoke, he kept focus on Rochelle, on how her gaze dropped low and flittered about the floor. "Maybe we'll have to deal with both guys at once."

"Now that's a chilling thought." Frank's sarcastic tone garnered a few shaky chuckles, none coming from Rochelle, who now lifted her gaze and stared back at Adrian, her wide-eyed expression revealing too much.

Fear or confusion? Maybe both. Perhaps she'd heard of Manzinni before today, but why so unnerved?

New in town.

From LA.

Acting strange…

He'd be negligent to say nothing.

Though his suspicions ran high, he forced a neutral gaze, not wanting to lose this woman's trust just yet. "How do you know Emilia, again?"

"Oh," she scoffed, swatting one hand in front of her face in a flippant gesture. "Same circles. You know, the local Italian community. Besides, her dad is a wealthy jewelry designer, my granddad started a coffee company in Italy that went international…"

Italian. Wealthy. And they know the same people… Emilia's ex-husband was the one who brought the syndicate to Harlow… Coincidence or connection? What better way for the syndicate to keep covert tabs than through a seemingly innocuous woman of means.

But he'd taken too long to reply and in the drawn-out silence, her stare hardened on him. "Who are you and why do you want to know?"

Though her sudden iciness sent him off-kilter, he let out a sigh and kept his tone casual. "I'm in Harlow to help these people shake the syndicate for good. So far, you've mentioned being in the same circles as Emilia, which seems to be the case with the syndicate, also. I hope you can see that asking is merely part of my job."

She shook her head and scoffed again, very much a headstrong heiress who didn't shy from confrontation. "I am *not* connected with any crime ring. I wanted a break from my travels and work, and with already knowing some people here, Harlow seemed a good place to stop for a while."

She twisted as if set to leave, only to turn around and level another heated scowl his way. "Actually, no, I'm not done yet. I take offense to your asking. My whole family has spent decades in this country trying to create something positive for our people. We give and give wherever we can. So, I absolutely take issue with Italians being constantly compared to criminals and crime gangs."

"Rochelle." Gordon reached for her hand, but she swatted him away.

"Oh, no. Don't stop me."

Gordon reeled back a little, perhaps never having experienced this side of his new woman. Meanwhile, water gathered along the rim of Rochelle's eyes, but the heat remained there, and she continued to stare Ramos down. "You're right, we Italians do have bad apples in our bunch, but did you also know there's a closer connection between poverty and crime, than there is to any culture? My granddad came to this country already a successful man, and yet, he still found himself locked out of opportunities, his business outright sabotaged, his ideas stolen... and still, he's a success story. What happens to the ones who don't have any of that?"

A tense quiet passed where he clenched his jaw and tried not to growl under his breath, even as his eyes felt like they were on fire from restraining his anger. That she accused him of being biased based on where her family came from. "You think I don't know that? My surname's Ramos, for fucks sake."

She nodded, still very much pissed. "Oh, I know you know, and I'm sure you understand that migrants often get locked out of education and chances to get ahead. Then there's the general distrust pointed at us. You know that only leads to us developing the same distrust right back. To communities building their own opportunities when the only other option on offer is failure. That's how gangs get started in the first place, right?"

"Right." He muttered the word because nothing she said here was news to him. He'd encountered the same push back in his own community. He'd worked within the same bodies of authority they distrusted. He'd experienced the in-built suspicion, could see through Rochelle's perspective, even if his own suspicions toward her didn't fully abate.

"I meant no offense." He peered up at her, surprised at his softened reply while still not sure he downright believed in her complete innocence. "There's more to us than the bad things that hold us back. So, I hope you and your family continue to do good things for your community."

The tension across her brow eased and the fire in her brown eyes cooled. For a long time, she stared at him in stillness, before she nodded to herself and spoke to no one in particular. "I have to go. I have some phone calls to make."

Eleven

LAILA STOOD within the doorway of her modest childhood home, her hand wrapped around Whitney's and the air outside already cooler. Not that a temperate evening mattered all that much, not when this house emanated warmth and love, and her childhood memories of bounding up and down the stairs with her little sister. Sometimes those memories lessened the sting of just how often she left Whitney here. That her little girl would create her own memories of this place and her grandparents.

Laila slipped the duffle bag filled with Whitney's things off her shoulder and strolled deeper into the living area, her mom standing behind the kitchen counter, while old Aggie smiled from above her teacup at the kitchen table.

"Working late again?" Aggie raised an eyebrow and sipped at her tea, the word "again" bringing a familiar pang to Laila's heart.

She nodded and gave a tight chuckle. "When don't I?"

"Oh, now"—her mother strode over and lifted Whitney for a quick kiss—"it won't be forever."

She *booped* Whit's nose and then released her. Whitney, as always, was quick to race upstairs to claim free rein over Laila's old bedroom. A room now strewn with way more toys than Laila ever had.

Even in Whit's excitement, Laila's reluctance to leave her daughter tied its usual knots within her tummy—a permanent, whispering warning that one day her greatest fear might come true, where something might happen, and Laila would be working far from Harlow in her daughter's hour of need.

Now, her mom drew in and landed a kiss to Laila's cheek, her familiar concerned frown taking over as she pulled away. "How are you doing, honey?"

"I have an assignment worth fifty percent of my summer school grade due the day after tomorrow, and of course as usual, no time to work on it." Laila fiddled with her car keys and shrugged. "I guess I'll study through my break tonight, then try to eke out more time tomorrow evening."

She wanted to lift her gaze to her mother but failed, certain her earlier worried look hadn't improved.

"Oh, honey. If I didn't have work tomorrow, I'd keep Whit here longer, but you're welcome to bring her back in the afternoon for an extra sleep over. That should give you at least a few uninterrupted hours to turn in that assignment."

Her insides churned that she'd once again be sacrificing more of her time with Whitney, but her mother's offer was a generous one, and as her Ma said, with any luck, this would all be over one day soon. So, she gave a hurried nod and lifted her focus back to her mom, only to glimpse Aggie padding over and her stare stuck to Laila.

"So, I'm about to head off too"—an unsettling glint spread through her blue-green eyes—"but not until Miss Laila here fills us in on that man from the wedding. A good deal of sparks were flying between these two, dontcha think, Vel?"

While Aggie turned her attention to Laila's mom—her actual name Velma—Laila bit her lower lip and held back the urge to groan, her suspicions on Aggie's glint all-too-correct.

"We just talked a bit at the reception, that's all." Laila mumbled through her rapid heartbeat, that beat a little faster due to having to lie as well as discuss Ramos.

Aggie's eyes narrowed, that glint of hers flaring brighter. "So, you two didn't have a date at the playground?"

Damnit! Harlow's rumor mill strikes again.

Laila curled her hands into tight fists to keep from slapping a palm to her forehead. She should have known Maureen Cooper, Harlow's very own walking-talking social media manager, would share the gossip soon enough.

And just to add to the discomfort of Laila's roiling insides, her mom's brows drew together, intensifying the depths of her concern. "You let Adrian meet Whitney already?"

"I mean, technically he already met her at the wedding, and he *is* our neighbor, so..." Laila went back to fidgeting with her keys, the metal clinking a fortunate distraction, though not enough to distract from the hot flush of her cheeks. "And yes, there was a playground date, but Whitney was only introduced to him as our potential friend, so I hope that everyone will be kind enough to leave the story there where it concerns her."

She lifted her gaze to her ma's huge smile. "But not where this man concerns you?"

"Ma, no—"

"Oh, my baby's dating again." Her mother clapped her hands together, a joyful rosiness coloring her cheeks. "That's so wonderful to hear."

Even though a smile tugged at Laila's lips, she made a point of holding a frown, not wanting to get her or her mom's hopes up. "It's been a long while since I was a baby."

Her mother shook her head and extended her hands to Laila's face. "Well, you'll always be my baby."

"I know, Ma." She leaned her head forward and tapped her forehead to her mom's. "Just don't get too excited, okay? It's still early days and I haven't decided what I think of this man."

"I know. I know." Her mother pulled back with a hurried series of fluttery hand movements that suggested she didn't heed much of Laila warning. "But aren't you glad I intervened with Whit at the wedding? With you so close to finishing your studies, and now this... Laila, you've come so far and have so much to look forward to."

But Laila's natural instinct was to tuck her mother's encouragement away where it couldn't hurt her. She hadn't forgotten the tension in

Ramos's rich brown eyes as she'd told him about Mike, or the gentle way he'd handled that first kiss. Oh, and his open surprise when she'd chased him down for another...

With her past, and the current danger of a looming syndicate, so much of that date seemed too good to be true. She could hardly remember ever feeling so lighthearted. So impulsive. That she even knew how to flit between vulnerable and having a little plain old fun, and in such a short space in time. Even if she never saw Ramos again, he'd succeeded in awakening parts of her she'd thought long gone. For that alone she could be thankful.

"Anyway." She cleared her throat and shook her head, bringing her focus back to her mom's openly optimistic smile. "Whit and I are a two-for-one package and that's a lot to expect some out-of-towner to take on. Especially since he has no children of his own. So, Ma, don't get all crushed if things don't pan out, okay?"

Aggie raised a brow on a look of total skepticism. "That warning really for your mom or is it more for yourself, Dear?"

Laila shrugged, a familiar swell of emotion taking up space in her throat because, in all honesty, she had thought through that same doubtful reasoning about a thousand times since her date with Ramos.

And as much as Aggie liked to cut to the core of most issues, just like always, her stark observations came with a sense of care over idle gossip.

"Yah know, you're right Aggie. I've been holding things together for Whit and I for years and sometimes I'm not sure how much longer I can hold on." She dropped her attention to the beige carpet at her feet and tried not to gnaw at her lower lip again. "Sometimes it feels like the smallest nudge might make me let go. I like Adrian. I like him *a lot*. But I can't afford the disappointment, yah know? So, as tempting as it is to jump all in with him, that wouldn't be fair on anyone."

"Yah, I do know." Aggie gave a steady nod. "Whitney was so young when Mike dipped out, and she had no idea what was happening when he left, but that wouldn't be the case this time around."

A dull ache burrowed deeper into her chest and Laila dropped her gaze away from Aggie again, the sincerity in her eyes only adding to the pain. "Not that I see Ramos as any replacement daddy for Whit, but the risk of getting too attached to anyone, then having my heart crushed… while having to parent Whitney… I'm not sure I want to put us both through that again."

"Well, maybe it's time to look at things a li'l different, dear." Aggie's rough and aged hand landed on Laila's shoulder with a gentle squeeze, a light smile crinkling the paper-thin skin of her cheeks. "You're a strong woman, Miss Egan. A great mom, too. But you're allowed to cut loose and have a little fun, yah know?"

Aggie pressed one eye shut into an exaggerated wink, and Laila gave a small and spluttering kind of laugh. Yes, she felt lighter for Aggie's cheeky suggestive advice, but perhaps this woman could have delivered it *without* Laila's mom standing right at her side.

But even then. Even as she twisted her gaze from Aggie to her mom, and back to Aggie again, the ache in her chest receded by a great degree. As much as Aggie called her a strong woman, as much as she'd carried countless burdens alone, she'd never been truly alone. She'd had other strong women surrounding her with good examples and moral support.

"Thank you." She leaned in and gave the woman a kiss on the cheek, followed by her mother, before backing away because she really did need to leave for work now. "Let's just adopt a 'wait and see' approach when it comes to all things relating to Adrian Ramos."

Twelve

THE NEXT MORNING, Laila once again sat in her driveway with her blank stare pointed through her windscreen. The light out there still held a muted early glow and the back of her eyes ached from her long night at work. As much as she wanted to, there wouldn't be much more than three hours to nap before her dad dropped Whitney off for the day and he moved onto his own work.

Resigned to not waste more time, Laila let out a sigh and stepped out of her car, trudging up her short pathway and then groaning at the effort of scaling the few stairs leading to her door. Her entire night had been spent standing at a mostly empty register or returning wayward stock to the shelves, and she'd somehow have to follow all that up with cramming in some studying while looking after Whitney. That meant entertaining and reading to her child, cooking, and attempting some kind of neatness in her home littered with toys and unfolded laundry.

"Never enough minutes. Never enough hands." She grumbled to herself and stepped inside her house. Next, she discarded her uniform in the laundry pile and pulled on a more comfortable set of home clothes.

Her next stop was the kitchen, where she searched the cupboards and fridge for what remaining groceries might provide lunch later, only for the search to end at the sound of someone knocking at the front door.

Bad timing. Super bad timing. She just wanted to crash and enjoy a moment of nobody needing anything from her, and still, she answered the door.

No one stood on her landing, and she scowled out to the quiet and empty street for a while, before peering down to find a rectangular, red ceramic dish waiting on her doorstep. She lifted the foil atop, the dish still warm, and two perfect rows of chicken enchiladas inside.

"What the...?" She raised her focus again in search of whoever left her food, only now noticing someone had mowed the neglected jungle she called her lawn.

A slow smile pulled at her lips, and she turned to Ramos's house, the man himself standing on his landing and smiling back at her. "I'd invite myself over to share that, but you look wrecked."

"Way to make a woman feel attractive. But thanks." She stood and chuckled, raising the dish in gratitude. "How fast did you have to run to get over there before I came out?"

Arms crossed, he shrugged one shoulder and offered an easy reply. "Let's just say, I now know I'm capable of clearing that little fence between us in one leap."

She threw her head back and laughed, only to think twice and cringed down at the fence. "You must be feeling lucky, that thing has pickets."

He chuckled and shook his head at her in a way that said he appreciated her wicked sense of observational humor, though he offered no words in reply.

So, she went about filling the silence, because frankly, she wanted to talk with him a little longer. "Thanks for the lawn too, by the way. You really didn't have to."

"What else is there to do while I sit about waiting for shit to hit the fan?" His expression lost all humor at his reference to the syndicate coming back to Harlow, and still he jutted his chin out to the dish in her hand. "I kept it light on the spice for Whitney, but those are my mom's not-so-secret recipe, and they were my favorite growing up."

"Not-so-secret?"

"Oh yeah, she's not stingy with her recipes. In fact, she'll write you an entire cookbook given the chance."

She pressed her lips together and held back another laugh, making a quick mental note on the endearing relationship this guy seemed to have with his mother. "I'll keep that in mind."

"Anyway, I hope you and the kid enjoy those as much as I do."

Laila gave a choppy chuckle. "Oh, don't worry, I'm sure we will. Strangely enough, Whit loves spice."

A small pause dragged out and she failed to hold back a yawn, one that forced her to turn her head to her shrugged shoulder to obscure her open mouth since her hands were full holding the dish.

Adrian straightened and uncrossed his arms, a concerned tension wrinkling his forehead. "You go get some sleep. We'll speak later."

She nodded, feeling suddenly a whole lot lighter for his help. As much as she had to do today, thanks to Ramos, she had one less thing to worry about. So, even as she turned for her door, she twisted back one last time to mouth the words, "Thank you."

Hours later, Laila sat before her pile of books at the kitchen table, Whitney draped over the couch in front of her favorite TV show, *Power Cats*. She'd already received a five-minute warning on getting ready for another overnight stay at her grandparents' house, but Laila knew from experience that getting this kid into the car so late in the afternoon usually wasn't all that straight forward.

The show's credits ran, and several cartoon cats danced about in various martial arts poses, signaling the perfect time for Laila to hit the STOP button on the remote beside her. "Okay, kiddo. Time to get dressed."

Whitney shot to her feet, like something out of an exorcism movie, and leveled a deep glare Laila's way. "I was watching that!"

"Yeah, and I warned you that we'd have to leave soon." Laila shrugged and walked the remote over to a high shelf in the kitchen Whitney couldn't reach.

"I'm *not* going." Whitney stomped her tiny foot to the carpet, the hem of her pink, cotton dress flicking out with the movement. "I've already been to Nana and Popo's house today. I won't go again!"

"Yes, you will." Laila set about refilling Whitney's water bottle for her overnight bag, aware Whit's temper had much to do with how much had already been asked of her today. "You're going to get dressed and I'm going to add a new set of pajamas to your bag. Help Mama, okay? Just for tonight."

But even as she strode over and added the bottle to the side pocket of Whitney's purple duffle bag by the door, her daughter's small voice whipped her back around. "Mama, I want to stay."

Her heart gave a tight squeeze at Whit's crumpled expression, and Laila sank to the floor, crossing her legs beneath her.

This moment, right now, was everything she'd never wanted. To pass Whitney onto family as much as she did. To argue over Whitney's desire for more time in her own home. As much as Laila felt the weight of her looming midnight deadline passing by, she extended her arms out for Whitney to come in for a cuddle.

Her daughter raced over in short, stalking steps, her head dipping into Laila's shoulder, her small body curling into a ball on Laila's lap. Laila kissed Whitney's shampoo scented curls. "Mommy wouldn't be the same without you, you know that, right?"

Whitney gave a few soft sniffles and nodded, her forehead rubbing against Laila's neck.

"And I know it's harder for you to leave the house at the end of the day." Laila dropped more kisses to Whit's hair. "It's not easy being a kid, is it?"

Whitney shook her head, her arms now reaching up to hug Laila back.

Laila responded by squeezing Whit a little tighter, suddenly not so eager to let her leave either. "I'll cut you a deal. You can stay in whatever you're wearing now. Would that be easier? Nana and Popo will be happy to see you, no matter what clothes you're in."

Whitney giggled, peering up now and quick to clap her hands over Laila's cheeks in fun. "Even if it was a scuba suit with a tutu over the top?"

Laila giggled. *"Especially* if you wore that. And just to sweeten the deal, how about I come over to Nana and Popo's extra early, and I'll make everyone French toast to celebrate you helping Mommy get closer to graduating?"

"Can I have chocolate spread on my toast?"

She shifted Whitney, helping her stand and using this conversation to surreptitiously get her nearer to leaving. "Absolutely. What do you think I should have on mine?"

While Whitney thought, Laila rose, pulling the duffle bag off the floor and collecting her purse from a nearby hook.

"Strawberries, maybe?" Seeming to not really notice the walk out the front door, Whitney slipped her hand into Laila's. "Do you think Nana and Popo have any?"

"Hmmm..." Laila ushered her out the front door and toward the car, each passing second fragile with the possibility Whitney might suddenly change her mind about leaving and the ensuing car ride might be filled with brain-splitting shrieks and demands to return home. "If they don't, we have bananas on the counter. I could bring them with me in the morning."

Whitney clambered into her child seat and began pushing her arms through the straps. "Yep. Yep. Bananas and honey. You can have bananas with honey on top, okay, Mommy?"

"Sounds good, kiddo." Laila dropped the duffle bag onto the floor beneath Whitney's dangling feet, her heartbeat slowing when she finally clicked Whitney's seat buckle closed.

Another step closer to getting that assignment finished.

After what felt like hours of coaxing, she sat behind the steering wheel, peering through the center mirror and smiling at Whitney. This would be a long night of cramming information and banging out words, and so she steeled herself with a deep breath and pressed the car's ignition button.

But the engine failed to start. All she heard was a painful silence. No spluttering. Not a single sign of life. No matter how many times she stabbed at the START button.

Trying to process this new hurdle, she paused her pressing, while a million fears collided within her mind. What if she couldn't get

Whitney to her parents' house? What if she missed the deadline? What if she failed summer school altogether?

Oh God, the literal cost of failing this course. Plus, the time added to her graduation date if she had to repeat this class...

She cut things close already just doing her usual juggle of being a mom, and a student, and an employee. The pressure of yet another thing to worry about threatened to crush her, but she was a mom, and falling apart was never an option. Especially not while Whitney watched.

So, she took another deep breath and forced a false sense of calm and rationality. She tried the START button one more time. Nothing happened. Nothing except her heart sinking deeper into her chest, but she turned to her daughter playing happily with the stuffed ladybird she'd left in her seat on their last trip in this car. Back when this blasted car actually worked.

Time ticked and Laila produced her usual shuttered expression, digging out her phone from her purse in the passenger seat, and finding something more productive to do beyond panicking.

"Who you calling?"

Of course, like most kids, Whitney had a sharp awareness of when her mom's phone made an appearance, often wanting to play with the screen or speak with whoever waited on the other end of any calls.

"Just Nana and Popo, but"—she waited for another ring to pass, hoping someone could drive over and pick Whitney up—"seems they don't have their phones on."

She hung up and tried not to release an audible sigh. Maybe she could call Ally, but that was an absolute last resort. Her sister was in the throes of moving in with Chip, the first exciting and positive thing to happen to her since her violent tangle with the syndicate. Laila didn't want to be a bigger drag on her family's fun than she already was.

But how long until her parents noticed her missed calls, or that Laila was late? They hadn't made any strict plans on when tonight's drop-off would occur, so best case scenario, it would be another hour before anyone maybe noticed and called her back, much less drove on over.

A groan worked up her throat, but she clamped her lips together and held onto any sound for her daughter's sake. No amount of fussing would make any difference, anyway. She'd only stress Whitney out. The car wouldn't start. Laila would lose a big chunk of study time —if she got any at all—and there stood a strong possibility she'd have to churn through Whitney's dinner and bedtime routine only to fall short and miss her deadline.

She pressed her forehead to the steering wheel, the frustration and fatigue from this day bearing down on her, though she made a point of keeping silent despite the heat gathering behind her eyes.

"Mommy, are you okay?"

She winced at Whitney's question and the unconvincing weakness in her tone as she replied, "Yep, all good, honey."

"Mommy. Look!" Whitney's sweet voice brightened and the distinctive thud of her bouncing in her seat filled the cabin, along with the sound of a hard tap against Laila's window. "Adrian came over to say hello."

Thirteen

ADRIAN'S tall silhouette filled the window of Laila's broken-down car and just like the fading sun behind him, she sank lower into her seat with an overwhelming desire to hide. He'd already mowed her lawn and brought her food today, and his presence now, in her moment of need, sparked a disconcerting pang of relief.

For a second there, she forgot her emergency. That she had a critical assignment due and needed to get Whitney to her grandparents' house. But *of course*, her car chose this moment to conk out. And *of course*, Laila's parents weren't answering their phones.

"Need help?" Adrian's muffled baritone broke through her rising panic, the man himself being just as guilty for her frazzled state as her defective car.

She hesitated for a second, recalling he'd arrived just as she'd been doubled over her steering wheel, visibly overwhelmed and leaving no room to claim she was doing fine.

"I was about to take Whitney to my parents' house for the night so I can turn in an assignment, but my car won't start." She gave a light shrug, and bit down to stop her lip from wobbling, her eyelids fluttering against the sting building behind her eyes.

His brow dipped at the center and his concerned gaze danced

about her face, as though he saw the farce behind her shrug. "So that's a 'Yes,' you do need help?"

Despite wanting help, just not from him, she pressed her teeth deeper into her lower lip and gave a reluctant nod. What other choice did she have?

He returned her nod with a more decisive one of his own, tapping at her window once more in a sign for her to open the door. "I'll watch Whitney while you get that assignment done."

She pushed her door open and stepped out, using the door as a shield between them. "I can't ask you to do that."

"You didn't, I offered." He paused a beat, his eyes narrowing as if he expected her to protest, but she was too dumbfounded for that, so he continued. "Between your fridge and mine, I'll knock dinner together. Set up your workstation in the living area and you can keep an eye on me while I do your kid's bidding."

Her jaw slid open, not just at his offer, but that he preempted and didn't belittle her doubts about leaving her child alone with a man she'd only met a handful of times.

"Mommy?" Whitney piped up from the backseat, jolting Laila into remembering her daughter could hear every word. "Is Adrian coming for a visit? Can I stay home?"

What to do? She frowned at Ramos, his brows raised in an amused look, while appreciation and guilt worked an unsettling course through her tummy. Yet another calling to take a leap of faith with this man. To accept even more on top of what he'd already given her.

His words about his past resurfaced. That upstanding people from this town had taken bigger leaps and trusted him with their lives... And still, a part of her wanted to say no. To deny him the satisfaction of her needing him in any way. Even as another part of her remained humbled by his offer and grateful.

She stepped back and slammed her door shut, keeping her attention down on the loose gravel while she rounded her car. "Just let me leave a message with my parents so they know about the change in plans."

Whitney made an excited squeal from inside, a squeal that didn't much match Laila's reluctance. Her stomach twisted in knots as she pried Whitney out of her seat, staring at Adrian from over the car's roof as she did so.

He'd been nothing short of her knight in shining armor here, and yet she couldn't shake the feeling that he would ultimately turn out to disappoint her. She'd experienced that exact same scenario with another man once before, only now her life was even more messy and inconvenient.

While Whitney skipped toward the front door, Laila left a phone message for her mom, and Adrian followed some paces behind, as though he sensed her need for space. Even as they entered her house, the silence seemed never ending, and he paused a few steps in from the entryway in a sign he took stock of the situation.

Not wanting to think too long on what he saw—a home not all her own, and lacking much of the colors or personal touches she'd like in here—a home very much lived in. There were traces of Whitney strewn in all corners. Randomly placed soft toys. Dented and worn furniture. Though Laila ignored all that and got busy opening her laptop on the kitchen table.

"Who's helping with dinner?" She flinched at Adrian's raised voice, but he strode into the kitchen confident as ever. And Whit, already low-key obsessed with the guy, of course bounded after him, shouting, "Me!"

In minutes, she sat on a high stool at the kitchen bench, just chatting away to him, while he showed her safe ways to use knives and peelers to prepare the vegetables for their meal, her giggles filling the air at his silly kid-friendly humor.

Not weighed down with managing her child, Laila raced through her work, occasionally glancing up at the scene in her kitchen, the same kitchen she'd shared with Mike. She would have given anything for him to engage with his daughter in this exact same way. It still baffled her that anyone could look at Whitney and not feel *something*. Or anything less than unwavering love.

But Adrian was not Whitney's dad. Though maybe she responded to him with so much enthusiasm because she wanted just that. A dad. Someone to share these mundane moments with. Because even her mother failed at that most days.

Laila gnawed at the insides of her cheeks and frowned at her fingers tapping over her laptop keys. Pushing down the guilt. Elevating the knowledge that she by no means looked for Whit's replacement father. One day at a time. *She* was enough. Any missed moments now would be made up once she could get a well-paying full-time job and drop her odd hours at the grocery store.

She kept that line of thought going until a good portion of her work was done and Adrian casually placed a bowl of baked pasta beside her open laptop. No crowing about his efforts. No requests for gratitude. No words at all, as he turned and sat next to Whitney three chairs away.

Just the uncomplicated act of making and serving food to Laila and her child.

Laila chuckled to herself and shoveled a forkful of food into her mouth, Whitney's chirpy voice introducing Adrian to the wonders of *Power Cats*, along with an invitation to watch with her after dinner. That's when he leaned in and whispered something in the little girl's ear.

Whitney crowed an excited, "Yeah!" before turning to Laila and proclaiming, "Mommy, after dinner, can I help Adrian fix your car?"

Laila leaned back in her chair and raised a brow at Ramos, "You're gonna get engine grease all over my daughter?"

He shrugged and turned to Whitney, "You won't touch anything, will you? Just watch?"

Whit gave a hurried nod, her eyes all wide and pleading as she shook her head at Laila. "I've never seen inside the car's thingy before."

"You mean under the hood?" Laila giggled and peered out the large front-facing window to her left, where she had a clear view of her car in the drive. Next, she looked to Adrian. "She stays where you and I can both see her, and far away from the road, okay?"

"Sure thing." He thumped the table lightly with an open hand, and then stood, taking empty bowls with him to the kitchen sink.

"Come on, kid." He collected Laila's car keys from the table beside her, patting her shoulder on his way past, Whit once again bouncing along behind him.

Her little face soon craned over the edge of Laila's car and onto the space beneath the propped-up hood, her eyes lighting with wonder, before she lifted her hands for Adrian to pick her up for a closer look.

Laila's heart squeezed as he did just that, the tension within her turning to a genuine laugh as Whitney tilted so far toward the car that Ramos had to wrangle her from falling out of his hold altogether. Whitney was so small, but comfortable in his arms, and he used his spare hand to point out different parts. Though Laila couldn't discern any words, she did grasp the joy in her daughter's tone.

She went back to work for a bit, until Adrian returned inside, Whitney still in his hold, before he lowered her to a spot just within the front door. "I need to stop by my house for something. Do you mind if I leave this one here for a minute?"

He pointed to Whit, and Laila shook her head. Her work was progressing well, and she could spare a quick moment. The entire time he was gone, Whitney peered out the door, her little body relaxing only when he jogged back from his house and took her hand, guiding her over to the car again. She watched as he put Whitney in the passenger seat and slid himself into the driver's side, mere seconds passing before the car's engine roared back to life.

Whitney's pitchy cheers sailed in from outside and Laila launched to her feet. "No way!"

All-too-soon, Ramos sauntered back inside with Whit again at his side, a wide grin on his face. "You'll never guess what the problem was."

Fourteen

"THE BATTERY on your key was flat."

Though Adrian did his best to maintain his smile, Laila kept blinking back, her feet taking her a few stumbling steps toward him.

"What?" The question fell from her lips limp and breathy, and she extended a hand, to which he dropped the key into.

"Easy mistake." He gave a matching 'easy' shrug, largely because her open expression of disbelief sent him off-kilter. "I figured the ignition or car battery might have gone but thought to test the path of least resistance first."

She shook her head and tapped the same hand clutching at her keys to her forehead. "Argh, all it took was replacing a tiny key battery? I feel like such an idiot." She lowered her hand, brows squished together in an apologetic look. "I'm so sorry for taking over your night and not thinking to check the fudging key."

He jutted his chin toward her open laptop. "You've got other things on your mind. It happens to the best of us."

He peered over to the kitchen, where he'd just cooked another meal for this little family, then to Whitney at his side and still smiling up at him, as though she'd been the one to straighten out the key fiasco. An adorable rascal if ever there were one.

Gratitude washed over his skin in a soft, warm wave. That he got to experience Laila's home and to help in her hour of need. Being a bit of a loner, he rarely felt needed. Not in any personal sense, anyway. And that she'd trusted him tonight. That meant something. At least to him. That she had faith in him around her daughter. That, on top of everything else, he'd had a real hoot just visiting in their little world…

Laila twisted around and her gaze aligned with her laptop on the table, her slowed movements hinting at an uncertainty he, too, shared.

In his hours here, she'd barely paused her tapping at her laptop long enough to pin much attention his way. Now that she turned back to him and held him in her scrutiny. Now that he'd served his purpose and fixed her car, his place here seemed suddenly less certain.

Not just in her home. In her life and perhaps in Harlow in general.

This wasn't his town. *This* was his work. But this place and its people were everything to her, and each interaction with him begged a question. Something beyond any issues with Whitney and her potential to grow attached to him. Laila had taken a risk on another man, Whitney's father, and to this day still carried the consequences of that bad bet.

And still, with every interaction, something grew between them.

But what exactly? Friendship? Respect? The beginning of something so much more? Whatever it was, he wanted to make taking a chance on him worth her risk. He wanted to prove he was more than a random stranger who'd barged into her life unannounced. And at the same time, he had little clue what his future entailed, so maybe he was exactly that.

Am I being unfair and hoping for too much?

She seemed more composed than moments ago, her gaze steady and a soft smile lifting the edges of her lips—an unexpected reminder of her small ambush-style kiss by the fence the other day.

I'm not the only guilty party here.

A quick chuckle broke from him at that realization, and he decided right then that this moment alone would be enough.

"It's getting a bit late." Laila extended her free hand out to her daughter, who gravitated closer to her mother as if by instinct. "Time for me to take a break and get Whit to bed, she needs help to fall asleep, so I'll need to go with her for a bit. I can release you from our house if you'd like?"

Though she held a lighthearted smile, the tension around her eyes didn't seem so sure; a doubt Ramos would leverage since her offered exit strategy made his stomach feel heavy and hollow. "I think I'll stick around, if that's okay with you?"

Her eyes extended off a small glint and she gave a small nod. Even as she pulled Whitney down the hall, Whitney peered over her shoulder to him with a frown, clearly not a fan of goodbyes or bedtime. Except, for a quick moment Laila peered back too, a wide smile on her face.

He worked hard not to make his return smile look too idiotic and then set about turning for the kitchen where the stack of dishes left from dinner waited for him. Meanwhile, Whitney's chatter sailed over from what sounded like an echoey bathroom, her words distorted, like perhaps she was brushing her teeth.

Things got quiet after that, and with the dishes done, he picked up Whitney's toys distributed across multiple spots in the living area and dropped everything back into a large, fabric-covered box already containing other toys.

The soft click of a door preceded Laila's re-entry into the room. Her silence and lack of steps once she entered caused him to turn and face her.

Her mouth hung slightly open, and her stare flicked from some random point in the room to meet his. "You tidied?"

Not wanting to make a big deal of his efforts, he dropped another toy into the box and shrugged. "If you're almost done with your assignment, I'll stick around a while so we can chat afterward."

"I have maybe another hour or so to go." Her brows lowered and a small frown pulled her lips into a straight line. "Are you sure you want to stay?"

"I've seen you through this long, might as well see how this all ends."

She laughed and headed to her laptop. "Hopefully, not in tears."

He strolled over to the couch. "Well, then, please tell me you've been hitting SAVE occasionally."

She laughed again, louder this time. "This isn't my first rodeo, kid."

She took a seat, her smile lingering on him a moment longer before she focused on her work again. Meanwhile, he settled on her couch and pulled out his phone, accepting a break from his own work to read the rest of the science-fiction novel he'd started yesterday.

A comfortable and calming quiet took over with the two of them centered on their own tasks, with the knowledge that Whitney slept peacefully down the hall. The hour passed quickly, before Laila's excited voice cut through the quiet. "I'm about to hit SEND. Are you ready?"

Her attention snapped from the computer, over to him, her eyes sparkling an exuberant blue. Her mood rubbed off on him and he sat a little taller, offering her a resolute nod. "Go for it."

At that, she raised a hand high in the air and made a slow show of descending a pointed finger upon her laptop's trackpad, before a soft clicking sound hinted she'd sent her assignment.

She took her hand back and slumped back in her chair with a deep sigh. "Want some tea?" Her gaze rejoined his, a little more serious now. "I'm so worked up, I need tea."

He rose to his feet and strode closer, following her to the kitchen, holding back from offering to make the tea because his help outside of emergencies seemed to only add extra weight to her discomfort. "Tea sounds good."

"Thanks for staying." She clicked her kettle on and turned to him, her back leaned into the counter and her arms crossed. "I'm sure you had better things to do with your evening."

"No." He stood just across from her and shook his head, that one word seeming to hold about all the explanation needed—which was none at all.

Laila's smile dropped and her gaze fell still on him, her shoulders drawing up and in, the firm line of her lips soon crumpling into a decidedly wobblier shape and motion.

"I'm sorry." A tear rolled down her cheek and she quickly used the heel of her hand to swipe it away. "This is so embarrassing."

Her focus fell, as if she couldn't bear to look his way anymore, her next words sounding choked and tinny. "I'm so used to dealing with this stuff alone and then there you were tonight, and I hate—" She thrust out a hand in his direction but seemed unable to finish her sentence.

Though a part of him said to give her space, he nevertheless sprung forward and took her hand, tugging her into his arms. "And I said it was fine."

"I know. I know you did." She choked on more sobs and her shoulders shook beneath his hands, thicker tears pouring heavy over the light dusting of freckles on her cheekbones, her sudden shift from excitement over getting her work done, to *this*... This uncontrolled outpouring. With the sense that all she'd held on to broke loose now the worst was over, and she had room to process.

"We went on one date and I don't want you to have to deal with the mess that is my everyday life." She leaned back a little and finally lifted her gaze to him. "You shouldn't have to deal with this. *All of this.* You're probably only looking for fun times and flirty chats, and here I am, already lumping you with babysitting and chores. Everything about this situation is pathetic."

Though her gaze veered away again, he raised his voice a little, vying for her full attention. "Hey. Look at me."

He waited until she did just that. "There's nothing pathetic about you trying to make things better for yourself and Whitney. And if you really think what I walked into tonight was a 'mess,' you need to stop a second and think about who you're talking to."

"You mean, because you're Dean's old war buddy?" Her eyes narrowed on him, especially as he shrugged. "You're really comparing my house to a war zone?"

He stayed silent, but yeah, that was what he meant.

"Oh, Jesus." Her shoulders shook with laughter beneath his hands, even as new tears rolled down her cheek. "Now I really do feel pathetic."

But the new light in her eyes contradicted that claim, and she dipped her head forward and rested her forehead to his chest, relaxing a little.

"You've been holding it together all afternoon"—he ran a hand over her hair and held her tighter—"this is just your emotions coming out. You're another step closer to where you want to be, Laila Egan."

She nodded in a series of quick and repeated movements, as though her emotions *still* had a hold on her, but keeping silent helped. So, he rubbed his palm over her back in soothing circles and did the talking instead. "In all honesty, tonight was a treat for me. A change in the usual way of things. And looking after one little girl for a few hours and swapping a key battery was a cakewalk."

"You also cooked. *Twice.*" She lifted her focus to him, eyes watery, but her energy less frantic. "This was too much. I asked too much."

"Cooking is another cakewalk, and for once, I wasn't doing it just for me." He took his hand and nudged her chin up to him. "See, one woman's 'mess' was this man's opportunity, and…"

He leaned in and dropped a brief, light kiss to her lips. "I can handle it."

A silence drew out where he leaned back to gauge her reaction. Where she said and did nothing but look at him, as though she sought to figure out things that couldn't be "figured." Trust wasn't something one puzzled through. Nor could he ever ask or demand it of her. Trust simply came in time. Even more so with this woman.

Her frazzled energy settled some more, and she sank into his hold, so he lowered his tone and reiterated, "I can handle it."

The confused strain between her brows slipped away and she lifted both hands to his face. "Thank you."

Her softer tone enveloped him. Not wanting to damage her trust, he closed his eyes against the uninvited wave of desire already swallowing him. Only, the heat of her breath brushed the side of his neck and his heart near burst at the lightest touch of her lips right there.

He tilted his head back and tried not to groan. Her body was pressed so close to his and her kisses failed to stop along the side of his neck. She tugged him down to her level, where her mouth traveled up to the corner of his jaw and across his cheek toward his lips.

That's when his hands snapped free of her shoulders and he allowed himself to cup possessively at her face, crushing his lips to hers and lifting her onto the kitchen counter, kissing her with all the fire already consuming him. If not for the chance of her daughter walking out to find them, he'd take Laila right here and now. Instead, he claimed a full and final fill of her lips, then used his last shred of willpower to pull away.

"Tell me you want more, Laila." His voice dragged out rough, gravelly, and unrecognizable. With all her strength and raw emotion, he'd never wanted a woman so much, and now he couldn't bear the thought that the next moments might end in any other scenario than having her under him. "Please. Tell me you want more."

Tension gripped low in Laila's body and her gaze stilled on Ramos. He wanted an answer. Wanted to hear that she wanted him. More precisely, wanted him now with her body and in her bed. So much time had passed since she'd last been with a man. That last time with Mike, and in a stage in their relationship so doused in negative sentiments. She'd simply gone through the motions of being with him in the naive hope that one day the relationship would recover. Clearly that hadn't happened.

And now, here stood Ramos, in a moment so *not* like that last time. Where need pulsated through her, and all she had to do was give a resounding, "yes."

Her overriding nerves made every muscle weak and shaky, and somehow that weakness felt good enough for her to offer a subdued nod. As always, Ramos read her well and dimmed his intensity by drawing in a softer kiss, his grip on her thighs gentle, as he wrapped her legs around him and lifted her off the counter.

She wanted words to break the tension, but all she produced was a light giggle, where she curled her fingers into his thick hair, while he navigated the corridor and guessed correctly where her bedroom lay.

And even as he found her bedroom, his passionate gaze held hers, and made her heart thunder with anticipation. Especially when he lowered her to the bed and pressed his weight onto her.

His kisses grew hungry again, strong hands brushing down her body with sure strokes that culminated in him tugging her jeans away. The sensation of hot, hard man over her left her senses exploding one-by-one. Even while she pulled her gray t-shirt away, his lips kept on finding hers. All she had on was her simple black, cotton underwear, but the fire in his dark eyes held her with an air of divinity. Like she was special and sacred. When for years, she'd felt anything but.

He melted her sense of self-consciousness. Surely a man as beautiful and alluring as him had his pick of young women with bodies not dented from motherhood. But no, he swept his touch over the curve of her waist, down the wider bulge of her hip, exploring her with delicate finesse. His gaze eventually fused with hers, and his next raspy words stole at her breath. "You're extraordinary."

Her heart squeezed and then leapt in her chest—startled in his admiration—that for this one moment she could be more than someone's mom. She could be a woman in her own right.

His praise had her surging up to meet him, had her hands working instinctively under his black t-shirt to the firm heat of his skin, where she sighed and proceeded to strip his chest bare, garnering his needy groan.

He shucked off his heavy jeans and pulled out his wallet from the back pocket, unfolding the thing to produce a condom, which he placed on the bedside table. Next, he growled and crept closer, only stopping when his lips met her collarbone, and his heavy hand took possession over her left breast.

She arched into him, pleading for more, and he kneaded her there, the weight of him between her thighs sending delectable shivers down her spine.

And still, she wanted more. *Oh, yes, she wanted so much more.* And his touch delivered. Tugging away her underwear, he caressed her sex, a surge of sensation forcing her to buck against him in an inescapable dance between desire and fear. Fear that being with Ramos may be more than she could handle.

But he'd already shown signs of being patient and accepting, so she focused on surrendering to this moment. With each of her slow and weighty breaths, her body warmed with a fire she hadn't felt before. She dared to reach for him. To take his thick and heavy length in her hand, seeking to affect him in the same way he did her.

He wrenched his lips from her with a frustrated hiss, catching her hands and pinning them either side of her head. The pace of this moment increased as he collected and rolled on the condom. A man in a hurry to stake his claim.

In all honesty, she didn't want slow either. Not this time. She wanted the thrill of succumbing to spontaneity, which was exactly what she got as he plunged into her in one firm and decisive stroke.

Years of involuntary celibacy caught up to her in a moan of pleasure and pain, his pupils dilating in a question, though she rose to capture his lips with hers, kissing away the uncertainty and whispering, "More."

From there, his movements intensified, and she sank into the sheets, relishing each thrust. He seemed to feed off her desire, his breaths ragged as he plunged into her, over and over and over again.

Each stroke built her need and forced her to arch into him, and she teetered on the brink. Teeter as she did, she subdued any cries of pleasure so as not to wake Whitney, her restraint only adding to the sense of this being a deliciously forbidden moment.

Adrian's hips rolled against hers and he took her with unforgiving force, her pleasure swelling like a flooding dam, overwhelming her senses and pushing her to gasp for air between each soul-shattering and stifled moan.

Bliss. For the first time in forever she felt unrestrained bliss. Her heart raced and her body shuddered, and a joy-filled sigh broke from her lips, as Ramos plunged into her one last time. He found his release and kissed her through the indulgent ebb of her desire.

She savored the beads of sweat over his brow and the spent flush over his cheeks. Stranger still, her body missed him the moment he pushed away. Even though he still lay at her side. Even as he pulled her into his arms and pressed soft kisses to her forehead.

"You're tired, Mi Amor." His chest rose and fell, and he stroked hair from her temple, while mutual reverence seemed to take over.

This felt good, but all good things ended eventually. Maybe she could be okay with that.

His thumb stroked a gentle line over her cheekbone, and he kissed her once again, like he read her concerns and sought to quell them. "Sleep now. I'll see you in the morning."

Fifteen

A SOFT EARLY morning sun shone through the window when Adrian awoke in the unfamiliar room, his first thoughts latching on the weight on his chest. *Laila.* Her glossy auburn hair fanned over his skin; her eyes still closed in her deep sleep. No doubt her last stressful few days had taken a toll, and then there was the sense that she never allowed herself to relax around anyone quite like she did right now. With him.

He'd never expected his offer of help last night to end like this, with him making love to her, and waking beside her in the morning. He'd expected to return home after Whitney was done needing him. But then came that kiss in the kitchen and the sense of this woman wanting to claim something for herself for a change.

A slow smile pulled at his lips, and he took a lock of her hair and ran the silk strands through his fingers. The morning's quiet and her uncharacteristic stillness suited her. Not that he could envisage her ever admitting to that. And right now, her soft, pink lips were turned ever so close to his and he burned with the dilemma of whether to risk waking her with a kiss.

He took the chance and instantly realized his mistake when her delicate taste hit his lips. Her sleepy groan only prodded his need further. She rolled onto her back, and he dared to run his hand over the flat of her belly, then lower still.

He pushed her thighs apart, her skin there already wet and hot and another soft groan invited him to explore further. So, he caught her right knee between his and held her open, swallowing her next gasps with light kisses that he moved from her lips and down to her jawline.

"Adrian."

He parted her folds and slipped a finger inside her, savoring his name again on her next low moan. She moved her hips in harmony with his hand, and he caressed her excitement in slow circles, her head tilting back on a breathy sigh.

He grew hard at her obvious need and the process of waking her. Drawing this out in ways he hadn't had a chance to last night was so inexplicably erotic.

And draw this out, he would.

"Why sonography?"

Her brow twisted with seeming confusion, but her eyes remained closed. "Huh?"

He smiled to himself, stroking her some more and earning her gratifying hiss of pleasure. "Why did you choose to study sonography?"

She gave a soft chuckle and ground against him, clearly wanting—but not getting—more. "You want to talk about that *now*?"

"Absolutely." He caught her lips for a long kiss, working languid strokes between her thighs, her knees straining against him as if to fend against her pleasure. "So, what's your answer?"

"I researched potential salary versus duration of study. Oh, wow —" She strained through a clear wave of need, then chuckled. He stifled a groan of his own, getting way too much of a thrill from watching her struggle through this banal conversation while he pleasured her. "Sonography seemed tangible given all the ultrasounds I had while pregnant, and if I had to study something, I wanted it to be something I felt mattered."

He dropped a quick kiss to her lips, reaching for his wallet on the bedside table for another condom. "Hmmm"—he rolled the condom on—"and when do you graduate?"

"If I'm lucky. Oh—" He'd pulled her onto him, her eyes fluttering shut, as he positioned her over his length. "Why so bossy this morning?"

Despite her question, her eyes sparkled, and her voice lifted with a mischievous grin. He gripped her hips and pushed down so that she sank over him. "You don't seem to mind."

Her head lolled back, proving his point. Having her like this brought focus to her neck's glowing white skin and the fullness of her breasts, her lighter skin color and softness an arousing contrast to his own body.

They shared a satisfied moan, and he cupped her, luxuriating in her feel. Both inside and out. Her indulgent curves spoke of a body that had created life, a detail that aroused him.

"You never answered my question." He gripped her hips and pushed her into moving over him.

"Oh, Adrian…" Her fingers curled into his chest. Her sighing tone a plea for release from having to answer.

But the thought of this strong-willed woman begging him for anything, much less release, only set his own desire alight some more. "How long, Laila?"

She stalled through a series of panted breaths, before straightening from her arched position. "A year. One more year, but only if I pass all my summer classes."

She tipped her head back again, clearly wanting more, so he gripped her hips hard and thrust into her, garnering her contented throaty cry, only for her to bite down on her lower lip as if to recall the need to stay quiet.

She flopped forward and buried her face into his neck, engulfing him in her feminine musk and the lingering fruity warm scent of her perfume, as she returned the favor and unleashed a series of rocking movements. "Do you interrogate your other women like this?"

"No." And he didn't want to think about any other woman, not with *this* one already in his hands and around his cock. The way she made his blood roar loud in his ears and every nerve in his body explode, perhaps he'd never think of another woman again. "Just you."

Not knowing what came over him, he held her in place and thrust into her, still unable to get his fill.

One night won't be enough…

He took what he wanted, and she moaned into the crook of his neck, only to nip at the thick tendon running down the side. He groaned with need and frustration. Maybe if he just kept going, they'd each get what they wanted.

So, he held her tighter still and pounded into her, his thrust wild and erratic, and increasingly desperate. More and more she tensed around him, crying her pleasure against his neck and dragging his own climax out into the open.

His hands clamped down and his fingers curled into her flesh. He was certain there'd be bruises, but she didn't seem to mind, in fact, her growing strain around him said that she liked it. That she wanted every last consequence for what she did to him.

And her soft whimpers, they spurred and stirred him. He arched into her until his own muscles strained and ached with the need for release, just as she clung to him tighter than ever and shuddered on a muffled moan.

And as predicted, even as he let go and joined her—his body erupting in a storm of building ecstasy and desperate longing—he knew a thousand moments like this one would not sate him.

He wanted her in too many ways. In ways he'd never wanted any other woman. Body and soul. And truth be told, his 'want' scared the ever-loving life out of him.

His heart still raced minutes later when the handle to the locked bedroom door shook, and Whitney's sleepy voice came from the hall. "Mommy, why's the door locked?"

Laila burst into buried laughter, and she jumped off him, stabbing a finger at her window. "Get your clothes and get out of here."

Even as the door rattled some more and he jammed last night's t-shirt over his head, she pressed a hand over her mouth and covered more laughter. "If you're feeling extra brave, you can walk around the house and knock on the front door and invite yourself over for breakfast."

Sixteen

LAILA OPENED the front door to find Ramos standing there wearing a warm smile and a wicked glint in his eye, ready to commence the game of pretending last night never happened. Meanwhile, Whitney's excited squeal filled the air, followed by the soft thuds of her jumping up and down. "Adrian's here!"

The levity in the way she called his name hit like a burst of sunshine on an overcast day, and Laila's heart gave a strong tug, an unwieldy smile breaking across her face.

She held his knowing stare since his presence was not at all a surprise. After all, he'd climbed out of her bedroom window moments earlier. Still, pretending he *hadn't* gave her a rare chance—in a town full of busybodies—to keep something to herself. Even though her priority lay in protecting Whitney more than avoiding gossip.

"Come on in." She stepped aside so Ramos could pass, then all three headed for the kitchen. "I promised Whitney French toast for her good behavior yesterday and I'm obligated to deliver."

Whitney's excited jumping kicked up another level. "Don't forget the chocolate spread!"

"I haven't forgotten." She watched Ramos open a cupboard door and retrieve a mixing bowl. "Oh, no. You've done enough for me already." She laughed and swiped the bowl from his hand, nudging him away with her hip. "At least let me make breakfast."

His overly still and perplexed stare somehow smoldered with the sense he wanted to lean in and kiss her... If not for Whitney being nearby...

And still, Laila looked forward to Whitney being here. To a peaceful morning together and Adrian's presence adding to the fun.

"Well, then I'll gather ingredients." He raised a brow, challenging her to stop him.

All she did was laugh and shake her head. "You can't help yourself, can you?"

"Can I help too?" Whitney peered up at Ramos, looking especially small next to him and in this cramped kitchen.

"Sure can, Chicken Nugget." He scrubbed her hair. "I need *someone* to tell me where your Mama keeps everything. Let's start with finding the eggs."

Since he'd already used this kitchen to knock together last night's dinner, he humored Whitney as she flung open the fridge and Laila tried not to wince at the crashing sound of the metal door hitting the cupboard beside it.

Seeming to take the crashing as a sign, Adrian moved quickly and shot out a hand, collecting the carton of eggs before Whitney could. He sent Laila a relieved expression as he lowered the carton to counter, and then asked Whitney if she could point out the milk and butter.

"We'll need cinnamon and vanilla too, right?" He looked to Laila again, seeming to invite her into his interaction with Whitney.

Though Laila clamped her mouth shut and nodded, she held back from asking how he even knew what went into French toast. She usually forgot that stuff and had to look up most recipes on her phone.

Just assume from past evidence that the man likes to cook.

Ingredients gathered, she began mixing everything together, while Whitney's cheery giggles continued through tugging Ramos between the kitchen and table, having taken on the task of placing napkins and utensils. The happy chaos lightened Laila's mood and her heart thudded with a realization that this moment, right now, was everything she'd wanted for herself and Whitney all along.

And there's no knowing how long it will last…

She left the bread to sizzle in a pan and watched Adrian setting down plates and glasses with Whitney, both chatting away while they worked. Such a commonplace image for most families, but one that succeeded in breaking Laila's heart. Despite *knowing* otherwise, she *felt* like she'd failed her child.

The emotion-filled tension in her throat had her turning back to the pan. Stolen dreams aside, she'd been everything Whitney needed. That was enough. That was something to be proud of.

A fresh kettle boiled and the cooking done, Laila ferried a plate of stacked French toast to the table, the aroma of butter and cinnamon well and truly filling the air. This *was* what she'd built her daughter. A house full of love and safety, and moments of fun amongst her hectic schedule. Adrian was an added bonus. *Not* the cure to a problem that only existed if Laila gave it permission to set roots in her mind.

Still, she couldn't help but notice contentment creeping in as they all sat around the table. This rare moment of calm in her busy life. A moment she didn't carry all on her own because she implicitly understood Ramos would help if needed. He'd pass her the juice just out of reach or cut Whitney's toast for her. He'd do that and so much more, just as he'd already donated his time and help because his friends needed him.

Because, despite her past experiences with Mike, the man sitting cross from her was a helper and perhaps an all-round decent person.

Once again, her throat constricted, so she turned to Whitney with a gentle smile and vowed to just enjoy the moment. "Good toast?"

Whit smiled up, teeth covered in chocolate, because, as predicted, Ramos *had* already helped spread and cut her toast. "Best day ever."

Though Laila giggled, a small hitch in her voice had her gaze snapping to Ramos, his smile dropping to a twisted frown as if he'd read her heartache over her long-buried dreams.

Seeming to recover, he blinked and pointed to a photo of Whitney at six months old situated on a small bookshelf a few yards away. "Who's that cutie?"

The photo featured her daughter cuddling a pink teddy bear, while wearing an oversized knit jumper and a mostly toothless grin. It stirred memories of another lifetime, one where Laila still clung to life's possibilities and things seemed simpler.

Adrian narrowed his eyes at Whitney in mock skepticism. "That's not you, is it?"

Whitney gave a big proud nod. "Yep."

"No way." He shook his head. "I don't believe that baby is you. Where's the big curly hair and where are all your teeth?"

"That *is* me." Whitney pressed her fists into her hips and gave him a sarcastic glare. "I'll prove it."

With that, she leapt from her seat and bolted out the room.

"Guess it's just you and me." Laila turned from the vision of Whitney's bouncing steps down the hall and shrugged at Adrian, catching his prolonged stare.

What went through his mind? Was this morning playing happy family too much? Was he having second thoughts?

Could she blame him?

"Laila?"

"Hmmm..." She refocused, not totally aware her mind had wandered, while playing at being oblivious to her likely obvious dip in mood.

"There's something I wanted to talk to you about." His pensive look deepened and her heart sank, as did her shoulders.

Here we go, we had our night together and now he'll hit me with a sad dose of reality.

What tactic would he go with? "It's not you, it's me" or "I thought I could, but now I realize I can't"?

And just as Whitney would likely re-enter the room, too...

"I know you said you'd given up, but"—he reached out and took her hand, the warm gesture sending a shock of confusion through her veins—"I was wondering if you'd like me to try to find Mike?"

"Wh... what now?" A useless creaking noise preceded her bumbling attempt at a question, her gaze darting aimlessly about his face, as she snatched her hand out of his. "Why would I want *that?*"

"Answers, I guess." He gave a tight shrug, his gaze falling momentarily away. "I don't mean to upset you, and I'm sorry if I already have, but you wouldn't have to talk to him, and he won't even know that I'm looking for him. What you might get out of this is that you'll finally know what happened. You'll be able to give Whitney some answers when she's older. Maybe contact him should you really need to one day."

Though her mouth hung loose, at least the fear of being post-sex dumped faded. Now her mind worked through the repercussions of what he'd just proposed. Truth be told, she didn't know if or when she'd ever need to contact Mike again. Nor did she ever want to. But Adrian had a point. She had next to no family medical history for Mike's side, and maybe, for Whitney's sake, she would need that information. And yes, it would be nice to have at least something to share with Whitney when she got older and developed a potential desire for more details on her father.

"Go for it." She snapped her mouth shut, a little surprised at the certainty in her tone.

"Are you sure?" Deep lines formed between his brow, hinting at his own doubts. "I've done investigative jobs before and sometimes the news isn't what the client wants to hear."

She shrugged, his warning still working to weigh on her. "Can't be much worse than being ditched with a baby and not knowing why."

His eyes narrowed just a little, again suggesting reluctance to believe her, his hand sliding across the table as if to console her, just before he stopped short of touching her, his attention snapping to his left.

"Look!" Whitney bound into the room, her voice an excited shriek as she waved the big, pink bear from the photo in her hand. "See, I *am* the baby in the picture!"

Ramos peered back to Laila with a somber look, before pasting on a smile and turning to Whitney. "Well, now, so you are."

Whitney grinned and skipped over to her seat again, placing the teddy in the chair next to her and lifting her glass of orange juice to the bear's mouth in a pretend sip.

Just then, a knock came from the front door, startling Laila even though she was quick to get up and answer it, the entire time regretting the broken moment. A beautiful woman stood on her landing dressed in what appeared to be an expensive emerald and white dress with a floaty, knee-length hem.

The woman looked vaguely familiar, and Laila tried not to squint in a quest to place where she'd seen her before. "Can I help you?"

The woman held a long pause, her stare scrunching with confusion, before a frown took over and she peered about her. "Hi, I'm sorry. I'm Rochelle, Emilia's friend from out of town. I'm told a man lives next door to you, Ramos, but he's not answering and I wondered if you'd know where he might be. I really need to speak with him."

The lady met Laila's gaze again, lips twisted in a small sign of nerves, though she shrugged one shoulder as if to hide the fact. "I see a car in his drive, I figured it wouldn't hurt to ask."

"Rochelle?"

Though Laila took the chance to be the one to frown, Adrian squeezed in at her side, his quick familiarity with this woman tweaking something within her.

She didn't want to fall into stereotypical jealousy, except here she stood, still looking ruffled from Whitney's hurried awakening this morning, and there Rochelle stood, so well put-together and a little too eager to speak to Adrian…

Rochelle's gaze rose to Adrian's taller frame beside Laila, then dropped to Laila again. "Oh, I'm so sorry, I didn't mean to interrupt—"

Laila grumbled and made to leave. "It's fine. You two talk."

"No, stay." Rochelle's voice shot out, and when Laila turned back, the woman extended a hand but didn't go so far as to touch her. "Everyone will know soon enough."

Her brows squeezed together, and she refocused on Ramos. "I came to apologize for snapping at you the other night at Maynard's. The conversation you were all having about the syndicate freaked me out, and something you said compelled me to do a bit of digging. It seems… it seems… Oh, I'm so sorry. I don't know how to say this…"

She bit her lower lip and squeezed her eyes shut, as though whatever she had to say couldn't be said while looking anyone in the eye. Except, just at that moment, Adrian's phone began to ring, and when he pulled it out from his jeans pocket, Dean's name appeared on the screen.

Adrian cradled the phone in his hand, but his deep frown stayed on Rochelle. Though she still gnawed on her lower lip, she jutted her chin toward him, before saying, "Go ahead, answer it. I'll wait."

Adrian did just that, his brows drawing tighter together, as he mumbled a few words of understanding back at Dean, his attention veering up and to the distance, in the direction of town.

Laila followed his line of sight, to a point where the otherwise clear sky looked hazy, though she formed no real thought about that because by then, Adrian had ended his call, his attention still fused on Rochelle.

"Can this wait? I'm needed elsewhere." He pulled Laila in and landed a quick kiss to her forehead, before brushing past Rochelle on the landing. "Seems the general store is on fire."

Seventeen

RAMOS GATHERED with the other bystanders outside the aftermath of the fire at the Coopers' store. Smoke still twisted in small spirals in the air and an oppressive smell wafted from the century old wood and brick structure, now reduced to a pile of charred beams and collapsed metal shelves. Maureen clung to her husband's arm, her unblinking gaze fixed on the rubble, while tears glistened over her age and grief-weathered face.

The townspeople around him were similarly shaken, some silent in their staring, others sniffling back tears, a few offering words of comfort to those nearby. Meanwhile, for some reason, Rochelle had followed him here. As if what she'd come to his house to tell him simply *couldn't* wait. Only now, even though she didn't really know the Coopers, she seemed just as shellshocked. Her face was a mix of wide-eyed terror and her cheeks about as gray as the smoke wafting from the decimated store.

Though he had little doubt the fire had something to do with the syndicate and the Coopers' refusal to sell, his mind still raced for more answers. Unfortunately, investigating these things took time. Time he didn't have. The kicker in this whole thing was that there remained no telling how many more lives would be ruined in the process.

One thing was certain. Harlow had entered a new world. A new era. One filled with heightened danger, where life as they'd known it ended. Mysterious LLCs were buying out businesses or destroying the property and livelihoods of those who refused to obey. From now on, no one got a choice over whether they were involved. The syndicate could pick anyone, and no one was safe.

By late evening, news of the fire had become common knowledge, and town hall filled to capacity with locals wanting answers. Laila sat amongst the fray of creaking chairs, clearing throats, and echoey whispers, the sheriff out front already addressing a line of questions in his usual measured tone.

"We have roadblocks set up on each end of town, as well as a few checkpoints throughout." His jaw hardened as if he hated being here just about as much as anyone else. "I'm sorry for any inconvenience on that front, but we need to be clear on who is coming in and out of this town in order to keep the syndicate at bay. We will, of course, continue to monitor and reassess the situation."

An audible grumble spread through the room, and she glanced back just in time for one of her old high school classmates, Lenny Brooks, to stand, his face already red and crumpled. "I'd leave this hell hole if not for all this syndicate bullshit making my property unsellable."

His abrasive shout jolted her where she sat, making her glad someone had had the foresight to organize a separate monitored room for the children to play while the parents attended this meeting, Whitney being one of those children.

Of course, Lenny wasn't done, and he threw his hands out to gesture at the people around him. "Now this? The syndicate has no beef with me or most people in Harlow, so why not ship off all the people attracting the trouble? A good few of 'em aren't even from this town, anyway."

His gaze skimmed the crowd, perhaps searching out Dean, Emilia, and Adrian. The out-of-towners he no doubt referred to.

"Sir, I understand your frustration." The sheriff paused to clear his throat amongst the inordinate silence that now enfolded this packed room. "But these are only precautions to protect the safety of everyone here. Sending anyone away is disproportionate to the issue at hand, nor is it a guarantee of peace around here. So—"

"Lenny's right." Another former school acquaintance, Gerry Gibbons, rose, his face set in a similar hard scowl to Lenny's. "Get rid of those people and the syndicate will have no reason to trouble the rest of us. Emilia, Blaine, Dean, the Overtons, the Egans, too. Oh, and that guy"—he stabbed a finger to the front where Ramos sat. Though too many sat ahead of her to view Adrian's reaction, she imagined him not giving much of anything away. "Get rid of them all."

Gerry's casual shrug made her body tensed all over. That she and Whitney were Egans too. That he could be so indifferent about tossing them out of town. That the room's energy had changed into what could only be described as a heavy moment of pause…

Are these people—people I've always regarded one step away from family—really considering his heartless idea?

She'd always assumed her place in Harlow as a God-given fact. As natural as having fingers on her hands and air in her lungs. The Egans had been part of this town for countless generations and never had she felt she didn't have a place here.

But how quickly could these people turn and how far would they go to assure their own safety?

Her face burned with the sensation that so many here potentially watched, judged, and rejected her. She wanted to run and hide. To uncharacteristically seek out support. From Ramos in particular. That said, Gerry had singled Ramos out too, and that had her wanting to defend him. To defend her family's right to be here too.

"Hey!" Before she could grasp what she was doing, her legs shot her to standing, the heat in her face now centered on her eyes and the stare she leveled at Gerry. "We are *not* the problem. The *syndicate* is the problem. And Ramos, for one, came here to help this town. So much for gratitude. I refuse to believe that you, and everyone else here can be so cowardly and hostile. We've all been through a whole lot of stuff together, haven't we? We supported each other in the past, why not now?"

Knowing she couldn't show weakness, she shook her head in her strongest expression of disappointment and disgust. "We're better than this."

Some people around her had the grace to dip their chins and avert their stares, a few went so far as to nod in agreement. She lifted her chin and stood a little taller, catching sight of Ramos and his soft expression. A mix of surprise and pride.

"Thank you, Miss Egan." The sheriff's voice brought focus back to him. "You make a valid point. We are all—"

"Screw that, I'm not taking any chances with my family." Lenny Brooks piped up again, stabbing a finger at Laila. "You got a kid of your own to look out for, don't cha? You know I'm gonna put me and mine before anyone else in this room. So, if the old sheriff here won't put his foot down, maybe me and some others will."

Lenny cut loose with a twisted grin, his gaze flicking over to Gerry, who nodded and smirked back—a pretty rich response given Gerry was well-known for stepping out on his wife and having next to zero cares for his three children.

Laila's heart sank and her gaze slipped instinctively to Ramos shaking his head slowly at her to drop the subject. And he was right. Nothing she could say would convince certain people in this town. Some would take matters into their own hands, even if that meant turning against their own community.

And, as much as she hated to admit it, Lenny was right too. She *did* have a child to protect. One she would, once again, be leaving in her parents' care tonight. She couldn't be there for Whitney all day, every day. Trying to match others' rage would only entrench deeper resentment toward her and anyone else caught in the syndicate's sights.

She didn't need another target on her back. Whitney even less so. So, Laila would go against her urge to defend herself. She'd sit back down. She'd stay silent. She'd do absolutely nothing.

Mark Farro read the email detailing the new roadblocks set up around Harlow and an unstoppable smirk pulled at his lips. He could just feel the drowning fear emanating from that town so many miles away. Each update offered new opportunities to adjust his plans in ways he would never have thought of. This one was no exception.

The blocks presented the thrill he always searched for. A challenge he could tinker with. Just when Harlow's sheriff no doubt figured he'd have Mark stumped. Those roadblocks gave him something to aim for beyond his grand plan of buying up the town's key businesses. Oh, he'd still make the place unlivable. Just in other ways. And the roadblocks would render these townspeople further cut off from the rest of the world.

He would be shut out, but *they* would be caged in.

Now, how to use this chance?

A new idea formed just at the tip of his brain, and he chuckled, even if he didn't yet have any concrete plan to hold onto. All he had was a spark. Just a spark. A *feeling* that this could all somehow work to his advantage. All he had to do was put the pieces together in the right order. That he would find other ways in…

He bumped his clenched fist to his dark wood desk, then shot to his feet, skimming his attention over the small office in this dingy, rented cabin.

What could he work with here? *A captive town.* He peered out the window at the cloudless sky. *The summer heat.* And, at least for now, he had the syndicate.

He couldn't get too confident. Not again. He'd been blindsided with defeat once, but unlike last time, he now had even less to lose. Not much more than his life and freedom. Everything else, they'd taken from him. So, he'd *take* too.

He'd take everything that mattered.

And maybe his problem last time was that he'd been too cautious. Maybe the key would be to strike and strike fast. *Bring his original plans forward.*

Besides, time wasn't in his favor on this one. Rudolph wanted his payback and Mark wanted freedom from the syndicate. And, of course, revenge. Though the question remained, how much would he be willing to sacrifice to reach his goals?

Making a decision, he stormed across the room and wrenched his office door open, catching Stix faithfully pacing the living room just outside.

The man's bald head and deep brown eyes turned to him. An invitation Mark took to put his plan in motion. "A new opportunity opened up, we have to gather men and we have to act fast. Get the other leaders on board. We have a town to destroy."

Eighteen

AFTER ANOTHER LONG night shift at the grocery store, Laila stepped out of her car and into the morning's eerie quiet. The memory of flashing lights from the new roadblock still hung in her mind, along with having to produce ID just to get home. She'd grown used to her routine. To this town's early morning hum and the tranquil trill of birds and crickets whilst most everyone else slept. But today, that hum sounded different. It sounded off. Or perhaps it was more the constant clash of thoughts in her head.

She steeled herself for the walk to her front door, to the added pressure to shut down the unease churning through her. Would she even be able to carry out her normal routine of having a nap or finding any kind of comfort before her parents came by with Whitney? One thing was certain, the Coopers' fire, followed by *that* town meeting, changed everything.

Her foot landed on the first porch step, where a folded sheet of red paper caught her attention, causing her heart to stumble its next beat. She clung to the hope that this would be another of Adrian's kind gestures. Kindness being something she felt deprived of right now.

So, she bent for the note, picturing his profound or romantic words and how they'd somehow succeed to settle her restlessness. But flipping the note open revealed something else entirely.

A hard and immoveable weight took up space in her tummy. There were no nice words. Not even a sign of careful penmanship. Only one unambiguous word scratched out in thick, black marker.

"LEAVE"

Her stomach clenched and she wanted to be sick. That someone came to her door to... to what? To threaten her? They offered no further explanation. No signature. *Nothing.* Just that one word. *LEAVE.*

She peered around herself, to the details of her porch and then the empty expanse of her lawn and the street beyond. As if her letter-dropper would have stuck around to gauge her reaction. But no one else was here. Only the morning quiet and isolation to deepen her panic and turn her insides stone-cold.

She had nowhere to pour her fear. No one to blame. Just hints on why they sought to scare her, while her sole certainty was that she would *not* be getting any rest now.

Her head pounded and her eyes felt overly dry, not just from fear or anger, but from her previous days of meeting assignment deadlines, entertaining Whitney, work, and now, severe sleep-deprivation...

Welcome to motherhood and the hellscape of living in Harlow at this particular point in time.

Feeling vulnerable and alone on her porch, she rushed to her front door and hurried inside, wrenching her phone from her purse as she walked. She had her mom on the line soon enough. While she clutched the threatening letter in the palm of her hand, a part of her still needed to confirm all this was real.

"I know what you're calling about and we got one last night." Her mother held a muffled voice, likely because Whitney still slept in a nearby room. "I've already heard from Ally, and she got a letter too. So did Sarah, though I haven't spoken to Emilia and Blaine yet."

"Seems someone's been busy." Laila dropped the note to her kitchen counter and squeezed her eyes shut, attempting to stem a rise of overwrought emotions.

She'd made so many sacrifices throughout the years, tried so hard to make positive changes in her life, and now it all came down to *this*. A group of self-serving men who didn't think twice to toy with a whole host of other people's lives, much less hers and Whitney's, as if either one hadn't already had their future altered by just *one* selfish man…

She let out a sigh and stared blankly ahead. "They're making good on the promise to take matters into their own hands."

"Oh. Laila." Her mother's tone dropped, weighted with a sense of sympathy. "With what the syndicate did to Ally, this is getting beyond scary. Maybe it *is* past time we leave Harlow."

Despite the rapid beat of her heart, a harsh scoff shot free of her. "And go where? Harlow is the only place any of us has called home and it's also the only place offering any protection. Who will stop the syndicate from tracking us down in any new hiding place? Who will help us or notice anything amiss anywhere else? They followed Chip all the way to Boston, remember?"

"I know. I know." Her mother's voice remained a tight whisper. "It's just that nowhere feels safe. Yah know?"

Laila bit her lower lip and debated stating that nowhere *was* safe, but a steadfast knock hit her front door and she turned from her kitchen. The tension pulling at her chest eased once she recognized Adrian's dark figure filling the space behind the door's frosted glass.

"We always figure something out, don't we?" Still, her churning insides held none of her word's certainty, but then, this was her mom and Laila didn't want to leave her on a hopeless note. "Someone's at the door, I have to go. Just tell Whitney I miss her and can't wait to see her again, okay?"

She and her mom said some final goodbyes, and then Laila hung up to answer the door. Adrian's worried gaze peered down at her, before sliding lower to the red note in her hand.

She stared across to a similar note in his hand, soon shrugging and putting on a dry tone. "Can't say the people of this town aren't thorough."

"I saw your car pull up. I came out to say 'Hi' only to find this." He lifted his note, brow still dipped in concern. "Are you okay?"

She blinked at his question, the answer being a firm *no*, though she didn't want to say that. Didn't want to give voice to her doubts, especially those pertaining to her ability to keep Whitney safe.

And then there were her thoughts on this man. That things moved faster than she wanted, during a phase in her life when everything was far from stable, all because she'd rushed things in the past. And even then, she'd always kind of had a sense of direction, something she didn't really feel right now.

Now, the syndicate wanted her gone, as well as a good chunk of people in this town.

So, no. She wasn't okay, and she wasn't sure about anything. Not about her future. Certainly not about Adrian Ramos.

That thought invaded her brain, just as her attention landed on his hand holding the note, her focus traveling higher, to his thick biceps and then his broad shoulders. This man was the visual show of strength she so sorely needed right now.

"Yeah, I'm fine." She paused and cleared the hoarseness from her throat, a sense of betrayal winding through her. That she wasn't being honest with herself or him. "Just a little shaken up, that's all."

His eyes narrowed at her, and he shook his head. "You're a bad liar, Miss Egan."

A small, but empty, smile broke from her lips. Despite the situation, she wanted to laugh, but she didn't go that far because his perceptiveness broke something more within her. "You're right, just... I just can't believe this whole thing is happening."

And even that wasn't the compete truth. Adrian's solemn expression said he knew as much. That *he* hadn't been self-serving when it came to her. Or anyone else in this town for that matter. He downright put his life on the line everyday he stayed here. In this town, and now, connected to her.

Unlike Mike, or the Gerrys and Lennys of this town, she couldn't see Ramos leaving her to languish.

And maybe that, too, added pressure to the prospect of relying on him in any substantial way. Too much pressure on him. Too much of a leap for her. A mother used to handling so much on her own. A relationship too new to trust when she had a daughter to protect, and a syndicate and irate townsfolk breathing malice down her neck.

"It's just people blowing off steam." The certainty in his tone broke her focus and he stepped closer, reaching out until his wide hand wrapped her wrist in a gesture of support.

A hot jolt ran through her body, and she lifted her stare to lock with his. She'd trusted Mike. She'd always trusted the people of Harlow, too. Did everyone always betray each other eventually? What made Ramos any different?

What a terrifying time to be an adult. Much less one in charge of a child.

"Thank you for checking on me." She forced a smile for his sake, her wrist limp in his hold as she debated snatching her arm back. "I appreciate it. I really do. It's just, they all turned on us so damn quickly, yah know?"

Her voice dropped to a raspy whisper and her heart raced at the intensity of his gaze. He drew in a little closer. The stillness in his eyes seemed to push through her attempt to downplay her worries. "That was a bold move you pulled at the meeting."

Her shoulders fell slack and her lips sank into a frown. "You think this is my fault?"

"No." He shook his head, his hold on her increasing in a way that added resolve to his words. "You stirred the pot a little, but perhaps that gave them a hint that we might fight back."

Her breath grew shallow, and he seemed to read her doubt, as he pulled her in and wrapped her in his arms. "There's still hope, okay? And you have to remember, whoever did this, it wasn't *all* of them. I'd wager it wasn't even most of them."

His eyes lit with an optimism that she didn't feel, and an unexpectedly boyish smile took over his face. One that shone a light on the ridiculousness of their situation.

Despite her darker thoughts on her relationship with Ramos and the turning of this town, a genuine chuckle broke free of her and she leaned her forehead into his, his peppery musk embracing her with welcome warmth.

"These things happen, Laila. People get riled up." He tipped her chin up and gave her a light kiss, his hand stroking all the way back and down the length of her ponytail. "With any luck, they'll feel like the angry letters achieved something and they'll move on."

Though she offered a weak smile, she sensed the conflict on his softened tone, like he knew their situation remained precarious.

"You can't promise me that things will be okay, though, can you?"

He shook his head, a small show of hopelessness entering his eyes. "You know I can't, but we'll try our best to get through this, won't we?"

Nineteen

THE NEXT DAY, Laila parked her car down the end of Main Street, the sheriff having called an informal meeting for anyone who'd received the red notes.

Venturing out of her car hit her with a hard dose of reality, or more precisely, the charred remains of Frank and Maureen's general store. The blackened debris seemed to stand as an unmissable omen of what was to come. As did her few short strides on her way to Blaine Callaghan's store, Oak Tree Furniture.

A few passersby avoided her gaze and veered their paths away from her. These were people she'd always been friendly with, but gone were the once expected smiles from their faces, any upbeat greetings replaced with frowns and silence.

She felt like a germ under a microscope and gladly partook in not looking at anyone right back, her experience now an indicator of what leaving her house would entail for the foreseeable future.

As always, her thoughts shifted to Whitney and what she would endure if the animosity didn't settle down. She started school next year. What if the syndicate wasn't gone by then? Would she be ostracized from all community events long before that, anyway?

Almost certainly.

Her hands felt shaky by the time she pushed Oak Tree's door open, her only relief being her first sight of Adrian as she entered, his eyes scanning the crowd behind her, having no doubt witnessed people dodging her on the way in.

Neither spoke, as they strode toward the small gathering amidst the living room display area. The sheriff added another calming presence, as did Dean and Sarah, Emilia and Blaine, Ally and Chip—all seated across a set of eggshell blue fabric couches, with a pale wood coffee table in the center. Laila's dad was there too, but her mom had decided she preferred to avoid the stress of this conversation in favor of looking after Whitney. Meanwhile, Aggie, Gordon and Rochelle, and the Coopers had been allowed to join since they wanted to help.

"I know you're all scared." The sheriff kept his voice low and steady, his gaze skimming over everyone, the wrinkles over his brow and the bags under his eyes especially pronounced today. "I don't blame you, but we're here today to settle on some solutions. The syndicate wants to scare us, that part is clear. They want us to feel helpless, which is certainly already the case for some in this town."

"Seems being 'scared' also works to set the closet vigilantes free…" Blaine shook his head, his arms crossed over his chest giving him a very unimpressed air. "Who also happen to be the same people who've spent years itching for their chance to play pretend heroes."

"Shoulda done something more productive with their lives than take up space at my bar then, huh?" Sarah scoffed and joined Blaine with her head shaking.

The sheriff leaned back in his seat, his posture suddenly taller, the move seeming to vie for renewed attention. "That may be true, but they're unknowingly playing into the syndicate's hands."

"You mean, by ensuring none of us feel safe?" Ally's eyes pulled wide with her question, her fingers curling tighter around Chip's hand, as though at any second now, she expected to relive her traumatic experience with the syndicate. Not that Laila blamed her for her hyper-vigilance.

But unlike Ally, who was the family dreamer, Laila was the realist, and she wanted to know the facts so she could plan accordingly.

"None of us *are* safe though"—Laila directed her words to the sheriff—"are we?"

The sheriff blinked at her for a few beats, the skin around his eyes wrinkling in a way that seemed to ponder her pointed approach. "We can't have people taking matters into their own hands, that's why we're here today. We need a plan and to investigate who's behind these notes."

"Just notes?" Sarah made a tsking sound and went back to shaking her head. "Oh no, this morning Dean and I found fresh roadkill on our front step. If I had to guess, it looked to be a squirrel. Wasn't a pretty sight."

Laila grimaced, only for her dad's uncertain voice to cut in.

"I didn't want to say anything, especially since I haven't even told Vel"—his attention bounced between Laila and Ally, his cheeks somewhat sunken in and pale—"but last night, at about 3am, there was some tapping on the glass of our front door. I went down to investigate, but by then, all I saw was an old pickup screeching down the road. It was too dark to see much detail beyond that."

Knowing her dad, he hadn't wanted to cause any concern, but the sheriff's deepening scowl spoke volumes on how Harlow's problems only intensified. He looked around the room now, his gaze landing on Adrian. "Do you have anything to add here, Ramos?"

"As you can imagine, most around here are somewhat suspicious of me." As usual, Adrian's demeanor didn't give much away, but Laila was certain his shoulders appeared more rounded than normal. "Intel hasn't been easy to get, but the obvious culprits would be Lenny Brooks and Gerry Gibbons. That said, I don't believe they're working alone. This is where it would be helpful to have a local on our side. Someone other than me or the sheriff. Someone, preferably male so as to appeal to the likes of Brooks and Gibbons. Our undercover local could perhaps gain access to any online groups being used to plan attacks."

The sheriff stared at the ground, nodding and seeming to think over the proposal. "I'll talk to some of my juniors, they might have some friends we can trust." He lifted his head and addressed Sarah.

"Failing that, do you think you might have some regulars at the bar who can keep a secret?"

Sarah pursed her lips and paused a moment, before replying, "Could. Despite their shitty actions, Lenny and Gerry still came in these last two nights. Come to think of it, they had a couple of extra people around them, too."

"So, not all that good at being covert?" Adrian rubbed a hand over his jaw, a hint of a smile breaking through. "I'll take that as an advantage we don't want to lose. It would be good to know their next move before they make it, at which point, we can make it clear that we don't tolerate bullies."

Laila resisted the urge to gnaw on her lower lip, her mind whirring with the knowledge that any further vigilantism could lead to an almighty showdown between two opposing sides. This town's existing chaos stood to explode into something else entirely, and through it all, she would have to protect Whitney.

Which means not sitting back and doing nothing…

"Any news on the syndicate?" Ally's voice cut through weak and shaky. "On Mark Farro and Rudolph Manzinni?"

Adrian held her gaze for a while, his jaw and brow strained in a clue he heard the ghosts of her past in her question and didn't want to add to her worry. "Yes, we have some intel and perhaps one small advantage. I still have ears to the ground and within the syndicate itself."

"With the help of outside agencies, we're making some headway." The sheriff eyed Ramos, hinting he wanted to add more." We can't reveal much as of yet, but I do have bad news, and this will heighten tensions in town further once word gets out. So, I need everyone here to be prepared."

"Hit us with the truth, Sheriff." Aggie patted Ally's knee in a show of camaraderie and support. "We'll handle whatever you have to say just fine."

"Don't be so sure, Mrs. McKey." The sheriff held a flat tone and took his attention away. "Just this morning, another business was sold to the syndicate. The gas station."

"Freakin' hell!" Sarah shot to a straighter position on the couch's edge and her gaze fixed on the sheriff. "You meant our *only* gas station? Why would Harry Jeffries do that?"

"The syndicate overpaid for the station and Harry saw an easy way out of town." The sheriff shook his head, one corner of his lip ticking upward. "After seeing what the syndicate did to the Coopers after refusing to sell, I don't like what Harry's done, but I understand it all the same."

"This isn't good." Dean's tone cut through with a dull edge of resignation. "It sets a precedent for the other business owners, which will hurt any residents unable to just sell and move."

"Oh, no, no, no. As if turning part of Maynard's into a makeshift grocery store wasn't bad enough." Sarah scrubbed her hands over her face and growled. "People will go downright bankrupt, while stuck in a town with no basic resources."

Laila locked gazes with Ramos, his stillness only making her heart sink deeper.

Imagine what will come of us when everyone turns to retaliation...

She snapped her focus to the sheriff and tried to keep a handle on one problem at a time. "With the roadblocks, fueling up out of town will be a nightmare."

"Town council is already secretly working on shipping in an alternate supply, but"—the sheriff rubbed the back of his neck and grimaced—"I wasn't lying when I said this was bad. If I'm being honest, we might not be able to hold off an angry horde for long."

"Well, angry horde or not, I still feel safer here." Rochelle reached out beside her and took Gordon's hand, an inexplicable smile on her face. "I plan to stick around."

A collective pause drew out and everyone peered amongst themselves with tight, perplexed stares. What a weird moment for Rochelle to choose to assert her dedication to Gordon.

Sarah's brows dipped in the center, and she craned her neck to stare at Rochelle. "Don't you have a stack of money and about a billion other places you could be? Why *are* you sticking around?"

Rochelle's mouth fell into a limp gape, her erratic stare bouncing about before she snapped her lips shut and mumbled some weak-sounding explanation. "I guess with all my travels, as well as being from a big city, I'm a little more used to danger. What I mean is, I like small town life and the people I've met there, and Harlow seems like a town worth fighting for."

Another pause dragged out between the group, and to be honest, the knot forming in Laila's tummy kept her from saying much. That's when the sheriff cleared his throat, vying for attention to return to him. "This new development furthers our need for a solid plan. And perhaps as Rochelle says, Harlow is worth fighting for, and we're not helpless when it comes to that, either. We have each other, and maybe enough locals on our side to keep the bulk of everyone safe."

In the sheriff's words rested an unspoken caveat. *For now.*

"Sounds like you already have a plan." Blaine leaned forward in his seat, brows raised in seeming interest. "Care to let us in on it?"

"Less a plan, more an idea. A real temporary one at that. Something along the lines of keeping hold of the situation with regards to the local unrest." The sheriff sighed, a deepened sense of wariness darkening his eyes. "If things should worsen, we would move you all to safe houses that the more malignant members in this town won't know about."

"Safe houses?" She sat taller, mind racing with thoughts of how she could rely on anyone else to protect her and her daughter. "Where on earth do we get so many safe houses? Much less places people in this town wouldn't know about."

"It's less about finding unknown locations and more about summoning all the allies we can." Ramos turned to her and raised his brow in a plea for her to drop her need to control every situation. To understand *this* situation. But control had been the only thing to get her this far in life, and fulfilling his wishes wouldn't be so easy. "Aggie has a guest house on her property. As do the Coopers. And Gordon has a spare room he's willing to share. However, we need more help, and those who'll open their homes to—"

"Wow!" Her jaw slid open, and she held back an incredulous laugh. "You have been busy."

Her laugh wasn't all she held back. There were her other thoughts, too.

You have this whole other life that I'm locked out from.

Which only nudged her doubts about how secure this relationship would ultimately be. The sensation of not knowing stirred deep-set memories of Michael and all the secrets he'd surely kept before leaving her.

Ramos held her gaze for a frozen moment. Her heartbeat slowed and seemed to pound against her ribcage. Though she'd always known about his work, that she couldn't be privy to every detail, she would have thought they were close enough that she wouldn't be hearing about something as intimate as her future living arrangements right now with the rest of the group. Why hadn't he come over last night to tell her? Heck, he could have at least called and given her the heads-up. All she felt was blindsided and unnerved.

"Laila, this is what I do." His hushed tone once again pleaded with her. "I know it's a lot to grapple with, but it saves lives."

He'd given her plenty of leeway and understanding, hadn't he?

Who was she to withhold the same. So, as much as the group held its weighty silence, she gave him a steady nod and hushed the voices warning her to guard her heart.

His gaze shifted about her face some more as if he still rightly saw her uncertainty when it came to him, then he turned back to the group, gifting her space all the same. "Make no mistakes, we're all in for a rough ride. If the safe houses go ahead, you'll all have to be extra vigilant that no one follows you to your new place of hiding. There'll be a set of precautions to take, such as concealing your vehicles within garages and avoiding any street-facing activity when in residence."

She clenched her teeth together and held back an urge to ask how exactly she would achieve that with a child who loved to run around outside. But even with that near-impossibility, what struck her most, was the crushing sense of just how much she and her fellow targets stood against.

Then there were the other overhanging questions. How much would their lives change and who would be left standing when all this ended...

Twenty

FOUR DAYS LATER, Laila sat at the kitchen table with her books sprawled out before her, her laptop open and a pen in her hand. She took notes for her next assignment, while Whitney sat cross-legged in the living room engrossed in the wooden doll house and dolls she'd received from her grandparents for Christmas. Occasionally, she would look to her mother and use a cheery voice to explain the imaginary happenings between her dolls. That, or she'd ask Laila to help craft dresses out of scraps of cloth.

As much as Laila needed to focus, she found it hard to dismiss Whitney's youthful imagination at work, and she smiled through the pang of sadness knocking about in her chest. Her daughter was growing up way too fast, and Laila longed to stop what she was doing completely and just get down on the floor and play with her kid.

That said, her thoughts on this peaceful evening at home were a far cry from the chaos outside, where the syndicate schemed and some townsfolk did the same. And her thoughts tangled on yet another complicated situation, her one with Ramos.

Though their relationship was yet another thing she had to juggle, she didn't consider it a burden so much as a confusing—but positive distraction—amidst a bunch of ugly events. And didn't she need more positive distraction? A relaxed evening and a chance to appreciate the good people in her life, before all hell broke loose?

She grabbed her phone from beside her on the table and then texted an invitation to Adrian for dinner with her and Whitney later. Within minutes she had a reply. He couldn't make it. He had work.

She sighed away her disappointment and reasoned that he had an important job to do. A job she downright appreciated since lives quite literally depended on him. Even if his work meant he couldn't and didn't tell her everything... Well, sometimes.

Wanting to shake away any twinges of sadness, she slid her phone away and stared at her books once again, her mind snagging on the last time Ramos stayed over. The way he'd held her, his lips always quick to find hers.

She wasn't used to feeling so seen or supported, and her body heated at the memory. Ramos was different. So very different from Mike. He was kind, and present, and he'd warmed to Whitney in ways Laila only ever wished Mike had. And unlike Mike, Adrian was here. Even if temporarily. Even when he didn't have to be. And she couldn't deny the way he made her feel.

She cleared her throat, as if that might work to clear her head, only for the distinctive thud of footsteps to hit her front porch. *Ramos?* Had he changed his mind?

Her heart leapt and her cheeks rose with a smile. The footsteps stopped and a soft rustling sound took over. Something about that sound snapped her back to reality. That whoever stood outside didn't pause to knock, and with all the antagonizing behavior directed at doorsteps lately, she would be a fool to make assumptions on who was out there.

Determined to be brave, she braced every muscle in her body and strode over to the door, giving Whitney quick orders not to follow. Soon, an icy chill pushed against her on the dark landing, that chill seeping deep into her veins, because no one stood out there.

All that waited was another red note shifting ever so slightly in the evening breeze.

At least it's not roadkill...

Anger had her pressing her lips together to stifle a growl, and she pushed the mesh door open, grumbling expletives under her breath as she bent for the note. Her belly soon rocked with sickness at the cruel words staring up at her. Yes, she wanted to cry, but she'd learned some time ago that tears achieved little, while actions could do a lot.

So, she stared into the murky dark and searched for signs of the vile note sender. A shadowy figure moved along her side fence to her right. Her hand shook, but she crumpled the note with her fingers and jammed the thing into her jeans pocket, while her better sense escaped her, and she stormed across her yard.

"Hey!" She recognized the tall but round figure as Gerry Gibbons and picked up speed toward him. "Don't you dare run, you sniveling piece of shit!"

About five years ago, Gerry had been a better-than average football player, but pity for him, he was much slower these days, while she'd grown significantly less tolerant of bullies.

Mere seconds passed before she closed the distance and leaped into the air, locking her arms around his neck from behind, turning herself into dead-weight against his next steps.

He twisted and twisted, swearing as he tried to knock her loose. But she wasn't budging and used the arm not locked around his neck to swing at his fleshy shoulders, kicking wildly with her legs and throwing in a few derogatory insults of her own.

"Who do you think you are?" She yelled into his ear, making this experience as unpleasant for him as possible. "I have a small child inside and you think it's fine to terrorize us?"

The audacity. Such a pigheaded *Gerry Gibbons* trait. Maybe no one close to him thought to keep him in check, but she sure as hell would. Especially given the nasty things his note contained about Ramos.

She kicked Gerry some more, not at all dulling the volume or rage in her tone. "You could spend the rest of your life trying to do better and you still won't contribute half as much to this town as that man has!"

"Fuck you, Laila!" Gerry swung around, dipping his left shoulder and sending her off balance.

No doubt he sought to knock her free, but the move did so much more than that as he stumbled and then fell onto her cold, hard lawn.

Her shoulder took the force of the ground, and he crushed her beneath him, just as a loud popping sound came from her shoulder.

Excruciating pain ricocheted through her body like a hot knife dragging through muscle, forcing a loud cry from her lips. She wriggled for freedom. So caught in a confusing desire to cause as much hurt as possible, even as she attempted escape, she still kicked at him.

Her heart pounded from the pain and agitation, everything about this completely unfair. Especially her aching shoulder. That her ability to work or look after her daughter would be halted because this selfish asshole just had to make her bad situation worse.

She yelled more obscenities and angry tears burned down her cheeks, her elbows grazed from the ground and her skin plastered in loose blades of grass.

In an instant Gerry's weight disappeared and the words "Get off her!" cut through on Adrian's booming voice.

She rolled onto her back and lay there gasping, her body wracked with pain, while Gerry stood over her, his shirt twisted in Adrian's hold.

His eyes blazed and he shoved at Ramos. "This has nothing to do with you."

"The hell it doesn't." She launched herself up and lunged at Gerry, only for Adrian to catch her shoulders, where she hissed through another wave of pain. Still, she held Gerry in a fiery glare. "This has everything to do with him. Your note says as much."

"What note?" Adrian shifted his hold to her waist, as though he now knew to avoid her shoulder.

Speaking of her shoulder, she peered down to find her left arm hanging at a loose and irregular angle. Though hot bile rose up her throat, she mumbled a defeated, "Never mind."

Gerry directed a slow smug grin at Ramos, indicating he counted her discretion as his victory. "Yeah, never mind."

"You know why I'm here in town. Whatever you're doing here tonight, has everything to do with me." Adrian's voice dropped to a low gravel, and he shifted her, so she stood behind him, as he drew closer to Gerry. "You're standing on Laila's property, and she's clearly injured. I don't take kindly to shady men trespassing at women's homes, but especially not when it's a woman I care about. So, tell me now why I shouldn't do to you what you've just done to her?"

Ramos took another step closer, while Gerry took a stumbling step back, his face taking on a trembling look of dread. "I didn't mean anything, okay? It was just a joke."

"A joke?" Adrian's voice turned cold, less a warning, more a stony promise. "It's funny to terrorize a single mother alone at home with her child?" He offered an unnervingly slow shake of his head, and Gerry backed away, hands held up in surrender. But Adrian's glacial stare didn't budge, even as he thrust an open hand out in her direction. "Give me the note, Laila."

New tears streamed down her face and her limbs started to shake. She wasn't scared of Ramos, but she'd never seen this colder side of him, and as much as she'd wished Gerry ill, she feared for him now.

So, even though Ramos couldn't see her, she shook her head and sniffled out the word, "No."

"Laila?" He opened and closed his hand, still not looking at her. "Please. Give me the note."

A long pause drew out while she prayed Ramos would change his mind, but he seemed just as stubborn as she could be, except right at this moment, he didn't have an injury chipping at his resolve.

She flicked her gaze up from her dark lawn and over to Gerry's glittering and fear-filled eyes. The man caught her stare right back, his smugness from before reduced to silent pleading. Ramos seemed to have nothing but time, while the growing pain in her shoulder wasn't going anywhere and begged her for relief.

Even though she didn't want to, she needed to end this, so she slipped a hand into her pocket and tugged the piece of paper free. She sniffed back tears, as she extended the note to him, his gaze only now breaking to read the page.

His cheeks fell a little slack, before he, too, scrunched up the paper and pushed it into his pocket, and lifted his flinty attention back to Gerry.

Sensing the increase in tension, she bit her lower lip and braced for whatever happened next, hoping against all hope things wouldn't get too ugly after all.

"Mommy?"

Everyone flinched and turned to the front door where Whitney stood pressing her body to the frame. Wispy curls pushed around her face in the light breeze and her eyelids pulled wide in unmissable fear. "Why is everyone yelling? Why does Adrian look so angry?"

Laila warred between running for her daughter and staying at Adrian's side, as if her presence might spare Gerry. But Adrian stole her dilemma away with a few quick actions.

He stepped back and looped his arm around Laila's waist, allowing her to lean into him, even though he still kept vigil over Gerry.

"Expect a visit from the sheriff"—he held still and gave Gerry one last intense glare—"and expect to pay this woman's hospital bills if you don't wish to receive a few of your own."

Twenty-One

"Maybe it's time to take up Aggie's offer of the cabin?"

Ramos watched Laila's resigned stare stay glued to the white hospital wall ahead of her, leaving his suggestion to hang heavy in the air. While he'd taken on the duty of bringing her to the hospital, Ally and Chip had stayed in Harlow to look after Whitney. The drive here alone took an entire hour, and now that Laila's dislocated shoulder had been set back in place, the time neared midnight as they sat waiting for a final x-ray to confirm she was okay to go home.

"I found out about Aggie's cottage being an option less than twelve hours ago." The pale, bedraggled cast of Laila's face spoke of pure exhaustion, and now her cheeks turned paler still. "Do I get a minute to gather my thoughts?"

The sting of her dismissal burrowed into his chest, but he guessed —or perhaps hoped—she didn't mean to take her frustrations out on him. He turned to her and offered his still gaze. She turned back and her haunted stare met his, the tension across her face falling slack. "Sorry."

"Are we going to discuss what happened tonight?" He paused, the image of her violent scuffle with Gibbons still fresh on his brain. "Or would you like to continue the silent treatment?"

"I'm not ignoring you." She twisted her focus back to the wall and spoke in a deflated tone. "I just don't know what to say."

"Well then, let me start." He shifted to face her fully. "While I appreciate the sentiment, I'd prefer you didn't get beat up on my behalf."

"I didn't get 'beat up'." She sent him a narrowed scowl denoting sarcasm, then returned to her wall-staring. "Gerry Gibbons, with his sucky sense of balance, landed on me!"

Not wanting to make light of affairs just yet, he pressed his teeth together, suppressing a need to smile at her description of how things unfolded. Though perhaps it was a good thing that, even in her exhausted state, she maintained a sense of humor.

He settled back in his chair and crossed his arms, resting his head on the unforgiving wall behind him. "Fair enough, but the point still stands. I'm here to protect you, not the other way around."

She sighed and mirrored his leaning, closing her eyes as she spoke. "Yeah, well, maybe I don't want you getting beaten up for me either."

"Laila, it's my—"

"Yeah, I know. I know. It's your job. I just... I don't have to like it, okay?" She pressed away from the wall and turned to him, her direct stare taking on rigidity. "And it's hard for me to sit back and do nothing, especially since Gerry stepped onto my home turf. And Whitney. Whitney was home tonight. And then the stuff Gerry wrote in that note. I'm allowed to get angry too, Ramos. I'm allowed to protect my own when some creep comes literally to my door."

"You think what was in the note was anything I hadn't heard before?" He scoffed and shook his head. The grim fact he'd become hardened to disrespectful comments made him the one to take his attention away now. "What's shocking to you is just another Sunday to me."

"Still doesn't make what he wrote right." Though he couldn't see her, her tone turned raspy, as though she absorbed the sadder reality of being him. That raspiness filled his belly with an undefinable tension.

Gerry's note had been filled with racially fueled hate. He'd questioned Laila's morals and shamed her as a "single mom" and "white woman" for choosing to be with an "immigrant Mexican man."

He'd then gone on to expand on the word "immigrant Mexican" with a slew of crude racial slurs.

Laila was correct in that what he'd written wasn't right, but being right didn't come at the expense of being safe. The last thing Adrian wanted was her getting hurt trying to defend him.

"Everything I've encountered in life so far has taught me not to be a passive woman." Her hand landed over his, and he instinctively turned his palm to connect with the warmth in her touch. "Whatever you and I are, Ramos, our few times together has meant something to me, and I care about you."

The warmth from her hand seeped deep into his bones, spreading up his arm and into the space within his chest. He'd never seen anyone get so upset on his behalf, nor had he expected it from this enigmatic woman.

"If that's true, then I need you to do what I'm asking." As much as he wanted to use this opportunity to mirror her affection, military life had taught him to prioritize his tasks, and right now, that meant protecting this woman he fast fell for. "At some point, the situation in Harlow might call for you to put yourself first, Laila. I need you to do that, do you understand? Even at the expense of me. Something like tonight, it can't happen again. You have to trust me on this."

He turned to face her, and her eyes were wide pools denoting something between adoration and grief. Hoping to quell some of her pain, he reached out to touch the soft skin over her cheek. "We'll find a way to deal with your more erratic neighbors. We'll take down the syndicate, too. It's all just going to take some time. So, until then, I need you to put yourself and Whitney first, otherwise I…"

He dropped his gaze away from her eyes, eyes that saw too much. Although maybe that wasn't such a bad thing. Not if what she read from him right now was that he didn't know what he would do if either of those two were hurt… Or worse.

Better for her to sense my feelings than to speak them out loud.

Something within him said she wasn't ready for any of that, and perhaps their situation called for restraint, too.

"Yeah, I know." He flinched at her voice, for a second there believing she really had read his mind, only for her small smile to indicate she merely referred to his order for her to stay safe. "I trust you, Adrian. I guess I just haven't quite learned to let the extra nonsense slide."

He gave a quick chuckle and breathed for the first time in what felt like far too long, tapping her chin with his knuckle to mark the lighter shift in mood. "I understand that, but maybe let me take the reins on this one."

Her lip pulled higher on one side, and she shook her head with a laugh. "You realize letting someone do that goes against every fiber of my being?"

"Oh yeah, I see that. You don't have much choice now with your arm all bound up like that." He nodded down to her sling, and she growled, pressing her head back into the wall once more.

"This is going to suck real bad. You heard what the doctor said, no work or driving for the next two weeks. I know I'll get through it, but I'd rather not have to."

He gave her hand a reassuring squeeze. "Yeah, but did you hear the part where, with this being your first dislocation, you got the best-case scenario in needing just two weeks for the tissues in your shoulder to settle down?"

She snorted. "Yeah, still sucks though."

He gave her that and let a comfortable silence fall between them, one where he allowed himself to get lost in his thoughts for a while. Predictably, his mind swung back to Laila's strength and courage, to her tenacity and compassion in standing-up for him, even though that wasn't the first course of action he would have wanted her to take.

The only other person to ever come close to having his back like that was Dean Holloway, and they'd been tight friends for over a decade ever since. He couldn't help but wonder if his bond with Laila could be just as long-standing.

That said, he couldn't ignore the clear battle she fought within herself. One of wanting to take on the world, yet not knowing how to step back and let someone else handle some of the struggle. Her trust in others was understandably tarnished. There was no saying whether she'd ever want to make room for him.

And because of her dented trust, and of what he'd recently

unearthed about her ex-husband, Ramos fought an internal battle. One that caught him between hurting her with the truth or fostering potentially life-saving hope.

He squeezed her hand again, seeking comfort for himself more than anything else, then kept his voice quiet within this small corridor and its bright lights. "You know, I was thinking—"

"Now, that can't be good."

He laughed and gave her a gentle nudge. "Shush, you! I was thinking that once you're healed, once all the syndicate stuff is sorted, we should go away somewhere. You, me, and Whitney."

Despite his casual tone, his heart inexplicably sank in the silence before she spoke again.

"What do you mean?" She lifted her head off the wall and stared at him, tight-faced and holding a confused scowl. "Like a vacation?"

He gave a disingenuous shrug and forced a smile, because hidden behind his pretense of wanting to give her something to look forward to, was the potential for him to stick around. In Harlow. In her life. "Sure. Just the three of us. Preferably somewhere warm."

Doubt flickered across her face in the form of her averted gaze, before she stared back at him, that doubt now vanishing beneath an easier mask. "Whitney's never been on a holiday. If I can fit time in between work and study, that sounds like a great idea."

A genuine slow light entered her eyes—like a woman releasing some long-standing belief, while still very much wanting to hold on— her pupils flashing their beautiful cornflower-blue. "And... I suppose I should consider us sheltering at Aggie's place."

He suppressed a jolt of surprise at her sudden change of heart, that she was actually willing to accept some help. "Even though you don't want to?"

She shook her head. "No, I don't. But Gerry's stunt might be the beginning of something much bigger. Mom and Dad are targets too, so I can't rely on staying at their place. I can't let my stubbornness put Whitney at risk."

He brushed a thumb against the back of her hand, then squeezed her palm within his in an offer of support. "Aggie's cabin is in the middle of a large and isolated, fenced-off field. Whitney will have plenty of room to play, and people can't simply wander over to your door like they can right now. I'll set up surveillance systems and alerts, so we'll spot anyone entering long before they get to the house."

"We'll?" She lifted a brow, her lips doing an inquisitive curl at the corners.

He smiled and gave an easy shrug fully aware he pushed his luck. "I mean, Gerry did single me out. You don't want anyone coming after me too, do you?"

"Ha!" She threw her head back in a genuine laugh. "Somehow, I can't imagine you being the 'run and hide' kinda guy."

"You're probably right about that." He chuckled and took his hand back, though her face was quick to fall into a slackened and somber expression. "So, the offer isn't really about protecting yourself, now, is it?"

His jaw muscles drew tight, and he likely mirrored her solemn look, the unspoken part of her question being that his presence would be about protecting her and Whitney. "Is that such a bad thing?"

She stared at him for a while and the strain around her eyes softened. "Not bad, no. Just... a huge leap of faith."

He paused before caving to his instinct to jump in with a reply, weighing his words carefully because, even though she had every right to doubt him, he didn't want her to doubt him at all. Not after all they'd been through already. Certainly not in light of where his feelings for her were determined to go.

"So, let's look at it this way." Seeking to instill confidence, he sat a little taller and kept his tone sure. "Your new injury means you won't be leaving the house much for some weeks anyway, and when you do return to work, your parents can resume babysitting duties at the cabin. I'll never be alone with Whitney, if that's something you're concerned about, and there'll still be times when I'll be busy working."

"Right, you'll have your life and I'll have mine." She pressed her lips into a thin line and gave a resolute nod. "Got it."

A hospital staff member stepped out from an adjoining corridor marked 'Radiology' and called Laila's name. She shot to her feet, taking a few quick steps toward the corridor, only to pause and smile back at him. "Looks like tomorrow will be filled with catching up on sleep and packing my bags."

Twenty-Two

LAILA PERCHED on the aged timber back step of Aggie's guest cabin, her focus trained on Whitney, as she skipped down the sandy path leading to the large, tree-lined field ahead. The setting sun glinted through the Jack pines to her right and birds chirped within the safety of this makeshift oasis, Whitney blissful and oblivious to the violence and hatred that had landed them here. To her, this was just a holiday.

Behind Laila, the savory scent of Adrian's cooking wafted through the screen door, the man himself occasionally coming out to ferry plates to the outdoor table where they planned to have a little "family" picnic.

Unlike her, Whitney and Ramos reveled in this experience, while she stayed rooted to her spot, nursing her three-day old sling and not at all sure this was what she wanted. She'd known Ramos just a couple of weeks, and here she was trusting him around her child and with her life. Her only certainty was that, if anything bad happened with the syndicate or the agitated townsfolk out there, she wanted to know she'd taken every opportunity to keep her child safe.

"It's okay." Adrian's voice preceded the light creak of wood boards behind her, before he sat at her side, Whitney still bouncing by the long grass ahead. "It's just us here."

He put his arm around her waist and pulled her in, prompting her to look at him. "Maybe that's my problem. It's just us here and no one besides Aggie for miles and miles."

Despite her protest over being an outcast, she offered a weak smile and leaned into him some more, his presence, in truth, helping to ease some of her tension.

He took a slow moment to eye her, then turned away to watch Whitney, the low sun illuminating his dark eyes to a glowing treacle color. "If it helps, you can think of me as your private bodyguard."

"I don't have to imagine. You *are* my private bodyguard." A genuine smile took her over. "My BWB."

He switched his attention back to her, brows slammed together in clear confusion. "BWB?"

"Bodyguard with benefits." She shrugged and looked ahead, trying not to cringe or laugh at her attempt at humor. Probably an early sign her brain wasn't coping with so much peace and quiet.

But Ramos gave her the grace of a chuckle. "Who in this town would ever guess that Miss Laila Egan could be so wicked?"

Though her cheeks burned at the truth in his question, she opted not to rush in with a quick reply. With all the new risks and this man taking up so much space in her life, she had this one guilty pleasure with him and didn't much want to run from her 'wickedness' just yet.

"You have more time to hit the books." His voice returned to a neutral tone, as though he sought to spare her. "Now that you have a live-in babysitter and no work to distract you."

"Babysitter, bodyguard... while my life's getting simpler, yours only gets busier." No longer liking her sense of habitual doubt, she reached out and pressed her fingertips to the prickly stubble over his chin, turning his face to her and offering genuine warmth in her smile. "You can stop trying to convince me now. I'm here, aren't I?"

She leaned and pressed her forehead to his, his expression easing, as his stare held her. "You better call the Little Poppet over for dinner before we make it really obvious I'm more than just mommy's friend helping out."

She chuckled and resisted an urge to lean in farther to kiss him, forcing herself to pull away, while adjusting the red summer dress she'd worn for his benefit and calling for Whitney.

The smell of roasted vegetables and grilled beef wafted from the table as they took a seat, Whitney quick to dig into the food.

"Adrian is a good cook." Whit spoke with her mouth full of roast potato and smiled at him through her words.

"I had a little brother to cook for and a really busy mom, so I learned young." He sawed into his steak but kept his attention on Whitney. "If you like, you can help me next time and I'll teach you a few things."

She gave an enthusiastic nod. "My mom is always busy too."

Quick to bite into a green bean from her plate, Whitney was unaware of the insult in her comment and a dull ache took up space in Laila's chest.

Adrian's stare fell on her, like he knew about her guilt, only for Whitney to pipe up again.

"Mommy?" Whit's innocent eyes glittered up at Laila, and Laila braced for whatever she might say next. "I don't like brothers, but I want someone little I can cook for, just like Adrian. Can we get a little sister?"

Laila's lips parted but no words came out, and her face turned cold, while she fought every urge to look to Adrian, afraid of what she'd see if she did. Whitney didn't know how little brothers and sisters were made, so the question suggested there might be some kind of 'sibling shop' Laila could just stop by and pick up a new family member.

Still refusing to make eye contact with Ramos, the chill over her face changed to a slow and stinging burn.

"Oh, Whit"—she reached out and gave Whitney's chin a tender pinch, embracing the sweet distraction of averting her child's thoughts elsewhere—"Mommy *is* always busy, and a little sister would make her even busier. You'd have to share me with the baby."

There! Conflict resolved! And she'd managed to reuse Whitney's comment about her busyness to her advantage.

"Ramos can take care of the baby and you take care of me." Whitney shrugged and popped more food in her mouth before she did the unthinkable and turned to Ramos. "We still have some of my baby clothes. I'll share those. We can all play with the baby and put her in pretty dresses."

Caught in a state of shock, Laila's attention veered over to Ramos, his fingers clasping his fork with a piece of speared meat on the end and his face muscles slack. His sudden stillness lingered, even as his blank gaze shifted to Laila and he mumbled, "She has our lives all planned out for us."

Laila dipped her chin and mouthed the word *no*, pleading with him to do nothing to encourage any new ideas from her child.

She forced a slow and cautious smile and dropped her gaze back to her daughter. "Whit, you're starting kindergarten next year, which is about as long as it would take to get a sibling. By that point, you'll have so many friends to play with, and some might even be happy to play dress ups with you. You won't miss having a little sister. Trust me."

Whitney's mouth formed a small frown and her eyes darted toward Adrian, as though he might help her. He thankfully did no such thing, and she soon nodded and returned to eating.

In a clear quest to cheer her up, Adrian directed a comically wide expression of interest at Whitney. "Watch any good Power Cats lately?"

Thankfully his attempt worked, and Whit lowered her fork, her entire face lighting up as she bounced in her chair. "Yes! Yes! Yes! There's a new season. It's so cool! Have you seen it?"

Laila pressed a knuckle to her lips, trying to stifle a laugh at the mental image of Adrian sitting alone at home willingly watching Power Cats.

He caught her amusement, his eyes crinkled in the corners, while he switched focus away from her and back to Whit, shaking his head. "No, but I wish I had. Want to tell me about it?"

Whit pushed loose brown curls from her face and straightened, as if making certain nothing could distract from the story she had to tell. "In the last show, they fought a giant robot, but they lost and got *swallowed*. So, then they had to answer a question to get out of its belly, but I already knew the answer because momma read it to me in a book."

"What was the question?"

"If I tell you, you have to think of the answer for yourself. Mommy and I won't help you."

Adrian gave a quick nod, his gaze flicking momentarily back to Laila, who didn't even try to hide her smile at his efforts to talk to Whit about something she very much enjoyed. Or that he'd succeeded in putting an end to the awkward conversation about siblings and babies. "Sure thing."

Whitney's grin grew impossibly wide, and she switched focus between the two adults. "Okay, here goes. What does a caterpillar hide in before it turns into a butterfly?"

He shrugged, like the answer would be easy. "A cocoon."

"*Wrong!*" Whitney squealed and bounced up and down again, almost toppling backward. Laila thrust a hand out and caught the back of her chair.

"It's a chrysalis, you silly!" Whitney stabbed a finger at Adrian, completely oblivious to the fact she'd almost cracked her head on the porch.

"Really?" He lifted his tone and jerked his head back in an act of surprise.

"Yep." Whitney giggled and nodded. "Moths make cocoons from mixing twigs and leaves around together." She leaned across the table and wrinkled her nose at Adrian in a lighthearted *'you should already know this'* sort of expression. "A chrysalis is like a shell and it's made from the caterpillar's own body. It's called an exoskeleton."

Adrian dropped his jaw open and turned to Laila. "What?"

She raised both hands in a matter-of-fact shrug, not even trying to hide any signs of pride over Whitney absorbing that little factoid.

With the dinner plates near empty and Whitney releasing a yawn, she took that as her cue to stand and address the table at large. "I'll go in and put together some fruit for dessert." She paused and looked at Ramos, already knowing what he'd say. "And no, beside you maybe stacking the plates, I don't need any help. I'll be back soon."

She gave Whitney a little wink and then walked inside.

As the kettle boiled and she washed strawberries using just one hand—admittedly not an easy task—she peered out to Whitney having swapped seats to be next to Ramos. Now, she cupped his face in her hands, the cupping turning to outright pinching his cheeks and pulling them into distorted angles.

Caught somewhere between intervening and letting him handle the situation, Laila laughed and ultimately decided to stay where she was. Maybe because he smiled through the ordeal, artfully keeping Whitney at bay with revenge neck tickles. And even as she laughed, something deep and aching shifted in her chest, and she had to pull her attention away from the giggling two outside.

The squeals of laughter hadn't abated by the time Laila came out to the table with a tray of sliced fruit. Despite orders to stay put, Adrian ended the tickle battle with Whit to return the dinner plates inside, bringing the two coffees waiting on the kitchen counter back out with him. Almost as soon as he sat, Whitney leaned her head to his shoulder and began devouring strawberries, her eyes slowly but surely drooping shut.

Ramos sipped his coffee and peered at Laila from over the edge of his cup, his narrowed stare holding signs of pride mixed with something far more smoldering.

Temperature rising and heart beginning to pound, Laila's body understood every word of what his eyes said, and she turned to Whit for distraction. "How about you change into your pajamas? You're about to nod off into a bowl of strawberries."

Whitney gasped and turned to Ramos as though she didn't love the idea of having to leave him. This act alone set Laila's nerves to a sharp prickle. This man and his patience had come to mean something to her and her daughter, and no matter how much Laila tried to slow things down, she simply couldn't.

Whit twisted to wrap her arms around Ramos. He held still for beat, his stunned stare on Laila saying Whitney's embrace was far from expected and that he didn't dare hug Whitney back without Laila's say so.

She nodded, and his shoulders eased downward before he patted the child on the back. For the longest time, the two just sat there in each other's arms like nothing else mattered but this prolonged goodbye.

Laila could just imagine Whitney outright falling asleep in Adrian's hold, but the child eventually climbed down from her seat and walked in shuffling steps inside, the unspoken assumption being that Laila would soon follow.

A hump formed in Laila's throat at how much lighter her views on life had become since meeting Ramos. Despite all the chaos surrounding her, and the pressure cooker of trying to stay safe, perhaps all that pressure gave rise to the sense they'd known each other much longer. The necessity to place trust in each other.

And who exactly had she sought to protect most? Herself, her heart, or Whitney? What Laila did know, was that her feelings for Adrian were new. They were exciting and so different to the last few years of pushing through each day. Mostly alone. He'd given her something she didn't want to run from.

So, even as she stood to get Whitney get ready for bed, her stare lingered on Ramos, his holding on her just the same. Soon, Whitney would be asleep, and Laila would have the rest of the night alone in this cabin with Ramos.

And maybe. Just maybe. She would allow herself to fall a little bit in love with him.

Twenty-Three

LAILA CRACKED open the door leading from Whitney's bedroom and into the darkened living room, her daughter now fast asleep. The newness of her surroundings buzzed with a low-level static, the stark quiet and lack of sun outside pushing her into a heightened sense of awareness.

The kitchen stood to her right, where the soft clatter of dishes and cutlery had filled the cabin as Adrian had tidied after dinner, while she helped Whitney to sleep. Another thing Mike would never have done.

The rushing sound of the shower down the hall entangled her in a surge of anticipation. She held her breath and ventured closer to the bathroom. Closer to Ramos and the promise she'd made herself about what she would do the moment she came out here.

The water snapped off just as she pressed her hand to the bathroom door. A door already leaking a thin sliver of light because he hadn't locked it. She closed her eyes and pushed at the cold, flat wood, her heart thundering at the hint that he'd known she'd come here to find him.

Sticky-warm steam enveloped her, and she opened her eyes to a light fog and *him*. Just beyond that fog. Standing before her in all his beautiful, naked glory. His stare didn't waver from hers. His body was ready. The silence between them only lasted a few beats, but time seemed to slow, before he broke the standoff and stormed toward her.

His lips slammed into hers and he scooped her up in his arms. His skin was wet. Not that she cared. She savored the sodden cling of her dress and the steamy heat of his freshly washed body. She welcomed his move to carry her and wrapped her legs around his waist, his lips devouring hers, as he took her to the bathroom counter.

Hard stone dug into her hips, but she savored that too. All that mattered was the way Adrian's hands claimed her thighs. The thrill of him pushing her hem higher and higher. The aggressive way he parted her legs and exposed her black underwear.

This small room was their own little world. A world inside a cozy cabin. One where her having use of only one arm didn't so much matter, because his undeniable desire filled in all the gaps and inadequacies.

She trusted that he would look out for her. *What a strange feeling.* Even stranger, that he could sweep her up in something so illogical and idyllic. They played house here. Played at being a family. And for this small window of time, she wanted to pretend all this was real.

His demanding touch brought her back to reality. *And what a reality.* One where he tugged her panties away and tossed them on the floor. She groaned. Caught somewhere between delight and frustration, which only got worse when he pushed her dress higher and growled into her neck. "This thing has been teasing me all day."

She chuckled and tipped her head back, expecting he might kiss her neck, only for him to capture her hips and drag her closer. She gasped, as he plunged into her, her next breath escaping on a satisfied moan.

He took her hard and fast, his hand pressing to the back of her head and driving her into an urgent kiss that spoke of something deeper than lust. She panted for air, but clung to him in search of more contact, her need rising to impossible levels.

He pounded into her in greedy reply. Every thrust ignited a new wave of pleasure that left her begging for release against his unrelenting kiss.

She couldn't take the pressure building in her any longer and nipped at his lower lip. He gave a frustrated grunt and crashed into her with punishing force, his desperation feeding hers, until she veered her mouth to the side of his neck and bit down harder.

He groaned and tightened his grip on her hips, as she clawed into his wide back and clenched around him. The pleasure-pain combination sent sparks throughout her body, and she released a muffled cry, even as she bit into him again. He threw his head back and swore under his breath, his shuttered eyes saying he liked this too.

He thrust faster still, riding out her release. She found space enough to lean back, but that only lasted as long as it took for him to wrench her to him with a growl that vibrated through her body. He gave her increased aggression, pushing her further and further. Like she'd had her turn, and now, he wanted his

Her body trembled around him. At his unrepentant command. At his inescapable need. A new climax built inside her and he engulfed her senses until nothing made sense. Never before had she wanted someone so much. Over and over again. Like every night could be just like this one. And she *still* wouldn't have enough.

That realization swallowed her whole and she melted into him, conceding he could take what he needed, because she needed it just as much. Maybe more.

He seemed to read her thoughts. Or maybe he mirrored them. All she could do was cling to him and gasp his name as he pulled her down with him on a roar of need and release.

He held her there for a while and neither one moved. Not until his chest shook against her on an elated chuckle. Like he reveled in the humor of getting so swept away with her.

She leaned back and gripped his face in one hand, repeatedly kissing him hard, gratitude swelling within her and compressing on her heart in a strange and achy feeling. She felt light and heavy all at once. Thankful for him. For this. For the levity he brought at a time that should be doused in misery. While a deeper part of her always questioned how long it would last.

For now, his arms still circled around her waist protectively and he gave no indication of wanting this to end. So, she happily stayed like that. Until his phone rang on the counter by her left hip.

She peered down at the thing and laughed at the bad timing, only to look back to Adrian and the new frown pulling at his face. His gaze switched from his phone, back to her. "I have to answer that."

Though her heart sank, she understood who he was and what he did, and gave a shaky nod. He kissed her one last time and put space between them, leaving the room and taking his phone and a towel with him.

Emptiness engulfed her and she stayed on the counter, just peering about and trying to decide what to do next. All she could do was adjust her hem and find her feet.

Adrian's mumbles traveled from down the hall. She followed the sound to the living room, keeping herself pressed to the hallway wall, truly not trying to eavesdrop so much as escape the loneliness of his sudden exit.

Attempting to drown out the details of his conversation, she caught a glimpse of him in profile, the towel he'd taken from the bathroom now wrapped around his hips. He held a worried look and scrubbed a hand over his face. His uncharacteristic pacing over the room's thick, shaggy rug, unfortunately prompted her to catch his final few words.

"Thanks, anyway. You're right, it's not the news I wanted."

Twenty~Four

"Has something happened?"

Adrian turned at the sound of Laila's shaky tone, her expression slack and denoting worry. He'd thought she'd stayed in the bathroom. Far away from him and the news he'd just received. But there she stood. Asking a question that was everything he didn't need right now.

"Not exactly." An ache formed in his chest because he couldn't bring himself to lie to her anymore, which meant the rare and incredible exchange they'd just shared was about to burst like an overripe piece of fruit.

Her brows wrinkled together, and she drew closer. The ache within him intensified. Time was up. When all he wanted to do was protect her from the pain that came with knowing the truth.

"Well, that sounds totally reassuring." Her voice rose with an attempt at humor, her ensuing small chuckle not all that unconvincing.

She stopped behind the fabric couch across from hims and leaned a palm into the back cushion, still wearing her alluring red sundress from the day. "Is it another work secret you can't tell me about?"

Her unrelenting stare bore into him and the heaviness in that look pulled his lips into a frown, meanwhile he glanced over to the giant glass sliding doors leading out to the back porch. Where they'd only tonight enjoyed a happy 'family' dinner.

So much for happy families...

Whitney had literally embraced him and filled him with his first taste of belonging outside of his own family. Then he and Laila made love with a level of honest intensity he'd never experienced before.

Wanting to maintain the peace, but aware he couldn't keep her from inevitable hurt, he released a sigh and gave her the benefit of his direct stare again. "It's not a work secret. It's about you and Whitney."

Her lips parted, before a more hardened air added tension to her face. "What did we do?"

"Nothing. You both did absolutely nothing wrong." He rushed toward her, set on putting out yet another fire, her stiff delivery hinting a suspicion he planned to cut and run. In one swift motion he took her hand and ran a thumb along her knuckles, making certain to hold her gaze. "I have news for you, but before I do that, you should know I'm not going anywhere, okay? Neither is my promise to protect you and Whitney."

"Has something happened in town? My parents? Ally?" Her voice turned impossibly small and husky, while the shadows forming under her eyes said his promise only added to her concerns.

"Nothing like that." Set on unleashing the truth, he tugged her closer and cupped her face in his hands, making her look at him. "It's about Mike. I've received confirmation on his whereabouts and movements over the last few years. You're not going to like what I have to share."

As if to shore-up her defenses, her lips formed a firm line and she pulled away, unbound hand coming to rest on her chest. For the longest time, she merely stared down at the patch of carpet between them, a million possibilities no doubt running through her mind, along with the dilemma of whether she wanted to know in the first place.

"Okay. Fine." She snapped her focus back to him and gave a firm nod. "Just tell me."

"Mike is still in Minnesota." That wasn't the worst bit, and he battled a desire to avert his gaze for the rest of it. Although looking away might give her the space to process the upcoming news, he wanted her to know he was here for her, even if a deeper part of him wanted to flinch from sharing the truth. "He lives closer to the city these days. He changed his surname—presumably to remain hidden—but still goes by Michael. Last month marked three years since he's been married to a woman named Nina Clark."

She jerked her chin back at that last bit of news, only to school a more neutral expression. "Oh...He moved on fast."

His stomach sank because she didn't know the half of it. "Laila. He also has two children. A boy and a girl."

"Oh. Okay." She gave a jerky set of small nods, her shoulders slumping, her cheeks baring a flush, while water came to glisten along the lower edge of her eyes.

A weighty silence passed, and she blinked at him a while before she eventually spoke again. "Is that everything?"

Laila's blood turned cold in her veins, all because Adrian shook his head, the muscles at the edge of his jaw seeming to take on extra strain. As though he braced to deliver the worst news of all. "No, Laila. It's not."

As if Mike living in secret wedded bliss, with two children he hasn't abandoned, isn't bad enough?

Her vision blurred and the world seemed to spin all around her. Too many emotions rushed in at once. Her lungs felt void of air, so she sucked in a new breath, Adrian's lack of reply perhaps more pain-inducing than whatever he had to share.

"I'm not going to like what you have to say next, am I?" Though she held his stare and rolled her shoulders back in a show of stoicism, he dipped his gaze down to the ground and nodded, the cabin's darkness intensifying the gloomy shadows about his face.

"You mean, worse than him building a life with another woman?" A derisive laugh shot past her lips, but the lump in her throat turned that laugh into a twisted sob. "Was I really so hard to lov—"

She pressed her lips shut, feeling far too exposed now to want to talk about love with Ramos. Or perhaps a part of her feared what he might answer.

His gaze lifted but gave little of his own feelings away. "I'm sorry."

"Just, don't say anything yet, okay? Give me a minute." She swiped at the fresh tears spilling down her cheeks and followed his lead at averting her gaze again.

She'd always figured Mike couldn't hurt her more than he already had, but here she was again, her agony unleashed and at the mercy of whatever other horrible secret he'd kept from her.

Wishing to break her emotional stalemate, she blew out a hard breath and began to pace a small area just ahead of Ramos, shaking her one usable hand in the air in front of her, as if that might release all the bitter feelings pinging around inside.

"What could be worse?" She muttered to herself but loud enough for him to hear, too. "He left without a word. Abandoned his daughter. Time and time again I've had to explain to Whitney why her dad went away, when all I could offer was a softened version of 'I don't know.' What could possibly be worse?"

Her tone verging on demanding, she snapped her focus back to Ramos.

His tight frown shifted from shock to concern, his cheeks hollow as he strode closer and caught hold of her arm. "Maybe we should stop here for tonight."

His voice was soft and soothing, yet she felt anything but soothed. Though her rising anger wasn't directed at him, she wrenched herself away, and deflected the internal sting from his compassion. "I need to know. I need to know now. I won't stop worrying until I do."

"Laila..." Her name was a low and gentle warning, but she shook her head, making it clear she wouldn't back down. His gaze shifted to the large sliding door leading to the outside world, just like he had moments before, perhaps a clue he wanted to be anywhere but here.

She couldn't blame him. Even when he cupped her face again and held on tight, releasing a sigh. "I had a hunch and was waiting on access to the birth certificate for Mike's eldest child." He paused, his gaze surveying her face, his tight brow yet another damning clue. "Laila, that child was born just six months after Whitney."

A sharp hiss of breath burst past her teeth, and she snatched herself from his hold in a stumbling step back. This news on Mike's eldest child meant he'd cheated on Laila while she was pregnant with Whitney, with no clear answer on how far back his infidelity really went.

Did she even want to know?

"I..."

I want to be sick...

Her mind flicked through memory after memory. The open look of shock on Mike's face when she'd told him she was pregnant. Of how he'd initially been almost *too* invested in her pregnancy, only to stop caring once Whitney was born. Every little moment came back to her in a whole new light. One where he was less an overwhelmed new father and more a conflicted man hiding a gut-wrenching secret.

For so long she'd figured Mike's laziness came from not wanting to be a dad. She hadn't truly suspected cheating... Or that he'd just wanted to be part of somebody *else's* family.

And the imaginary world she'd built in her mind about him in his absence—forever assuming he'd ruin every relationship succeeding the one with her—that he'd never truly commit to someone. That he'd waste his life away. *Alone.*

She scuffed her bare feet over the rough carpet and backed away, as though Ramos were Mike and she were a younger Laila, gifted a chance to make better decisions on how her life would go.

"How?" The question fell from her, again, as if she were speaking to Mike.

"Nina Clark worked with Mike." Adrian's hands curled into tight fists at his sides, as though he wanted to come get her and tell her everything would be alright. But the dark circles under his eyes told her nothing was *alright.* "The affair got him fired from his old job. The one he had when Whit was born."

A pitchy squeak slipped from her lips, and she clapped a hand over her mouth only to feel a wet new swell of tears washing over her cheeks.

How embarrassing!

All those times she'd scrambled to find money. To do *anything* to keep that man in her life. And although Mike worked a little out of town, no one from his old job had reached out to tell her. They'd left her to do the exhausting dance of trying to keep her family together, never really knowing the truth of what went wrong.

"Are you okay, Laila?"

She shook her head and stared at Whitney's closed bedroom door, heart a pain-filled mess beneath her ribcage, wanting nothing but to escape everything about this moment.

"I need her." She blinked at that door and reminded herself of something she'd always sought to keep in mind. That it wasn't fair to expect a child to carry a parent's burdens. So, as always, she shifted her perspective, lifted her posture, and packed everything away. Especially her torrid emotions. "I need to go to her."

All the hurt. All the betrayal. Every urge to lash out and be angry at the world. Everything got locked away behind an impenetrable wall she'd been building since the day she'd learned she would be a mother. That's what good mothers did, didn't they? They held every moment together. Especially the more painful ones.

"I'll sleep next to Whitney tonight." Her voice came out perhaps a little too calm. Too cold. She strode for Whitney's door, refusing to ask for permission to go to *her* child. Not Mike's. Not Adrian's. *Hers.* That child, the one constant that would never leave her. Her reason for not falling apart completely.

"I'll see you in the morning."

Twenty-Five

A WEEK and a half passed before Laila was given clearance to remove her sling long enough to drive to and from work. Now, she paced around the cabin's kitchen adjusting her sling and packing her lunch for her first shift back, her duties at the store limited to serving at the cigarette counter.

Willing her parents to arrive to watch Whitney, where they would take her for a sleepover at their safehouse for a small break from the confines of *this* safehouse, she glanced out the living room window. Ramos sat in her peripheral vision, cross-legged on the floor, helping Whit put together a forty-eight-piece puzzle.

He, too, had a work thing to leave for. As usual, something secretive, though in this case, her lack of knowledge was partly her fault. Every time his stare caught hers, she'd look away. An unfair habit she'd formed since learning about Mike's secret family. One she struggled to break.

The wind had been knocked right out of her ability to fully engage with others, especially Ramos, since he was the closest thing to Mike. Again, an unfair comparison, but then grief and trauma weren't always all that logical.

So, now she was trapped in a loop of constantly trying to open up to Ramos, while battling a renewed need to keep every heartbroken or inconvenient emotion to herself.

"Mommy's too sad lately."

Whitney's small voice jolted Laila from her thoughts, though the child had likely read whatever far-off expression Laila currently held. Her heart strained and she snapped her attention to her daughter, Whit's lower lip pouted in a frown.

Though she moved to comfort her daughter, Ramos got there first. "Everyone gets sad sometimes. Mommies too. Sometimes we all just need a little time to figure out our feelings."

Ramos turned his gaze to her, the steadfast look in his eyes speaking volumes. As much as he didn't deserve her shutting him out, he somewhat understood her reasons why.

She tilted her head to one side and offered an appreciative nod.

"Adrian's right." She crouched down beside Whitney and cupped her child's face. "And even if I am a little sad, sad feelings don't make me love you any less. In fact, when I am sad, guess who makes me happiest of all?"

Whitney's eyes lit up, as did her smile, those gappy teeth of hers working their magic on Laila's mood. "Me?"

"Yah betcha." Laila leaned in and gave Whit some kisses on her cheeks, nose, and forehead. "Every single time, Baby Girl."

Whitney flopped forward and embraced her mother, her little head coming to rest on her chest. Meanwhile, Laila lifted her focus to Ramos, reaching out to press her hand to his cheek. Her first bit of physical contact with him in over a week. "We'll have a talk when we're both done with work, okay?"

He gave her an understanding nod. She gave Whitney one last kiss. The shuddering metallic sound of the garage opening announced her parents' arrival, and she joined Ramos in standing.

Maybe she didn't know a great deal about him or his work, but she did know he was *nothing* like Mike. Ramos showed up for her time and time again, and in ways Mike never had. *That* alone deserved some of her trust. Or at least a second chance.

Her parents knocked at the front door, and she moved to let them in, only for Adrian to catch her hand and spin her toward him. While she remained startled, he pressed a gentle kiss to her forehead, melting away days of tension.

"I should be back before you return. I'm looking forward to that talk."

———

Around midnight, Adrian pulled his car over in front of a small cabin across state lines in North Dakota. His heart beat rapidly as he positioned the vehicle to remain concealed along the edge of some woods.

The outside world carried no signs of human life, just the incessant chirp of night insects. Keeping his movements as silent as possible, he cracked his door open and snuck closer to the property's perimeter, searching for a decent vantage point and somewhere to hide.

This was an unauthorized visit, a risk he took based on an unreliable tip-off. His skin prickled at the expanse of land between the cabin and the road. Plenty of open space for him to get caught, but with a small ornamental garden located yards from the front porch and a leafy lattice wall that could work as a barrier between him and whoever might be inside.

His protectiveness over Laila and Whitney had kept him from this investigation long enough, while another part of him feared he might succeed at cracking this small piece of the syndicate puzzle. If the syndicate fell, so did his reasons for being in town. With the shaky ground he already stood on with Laila, there seemed nowhere the relationship would go after that.

But he needed to put his personal reasons aside for the good of everyone. So here he was, huddled against a floral archway and focused on his job, searching for any signs that might put this whole awful ordeal to rest.

A set of cream curtains sat open in the front-window, the cabin's interior holding an expected sense of country-comfort. The egg-shell blue walls held many landscape paintings, those walls also lined with a couple of dark wood shelves stacked with books and decorative ceramics. Though his far-off position kept him from seeing much, if he were lucky, someone would walk past, and he would get confirmation his journey today hadn't been wasted.

That said, if confirmation took too long, he would have to risk venturing even closer. While he waited, he chanced a look at the driveway and double-checked there were no cars. Not that that meant much. The place had a double garage, but the lights on inside were a good indication he would get what he'd come for, despite the discomfort of cold nipping at his face. He would wait. *Hours if he had to.*

But just as that possibility crossed his mind, a man with a close-shaven head stepped into view inside. Someone who looked familiar. *But not his target.* This man stopped to peer through the window, his dark gaze sweeping over the world outside. Currently Adrian's world. Ramos held still, his hand instinctively dropping to his unclipped gun on his hip holster.

The man inside lifted his hands, grabbing the curtain's inner edges as though set to tug them closed, his focus still set on the yard. Just then, his stare locked onto Ramos. His hands paused. As did the rest of him. Though Ramos's pulse thudded loud in his ears, this man seemed to take a moment, as if weighing what to do.

Adrian didn't want to be the first to start a gunfight. Not when he was yet to spot his target. But the man before him was at least good enough at his job to have been looking for, and spotted, Ramos. So, maybe there would be no choice on that matter.

More seconds passed and the man kept his hands high and in plain view. A good sign that got even better as he tilted his chin upward in an admission that Ramos's intel had been correct.

Mark's men were tired of being pulled into his blood wars.

They sought to make a sacrifice.

The man inside dropped his hands and turned, leaving the curtains agape in an open invitation for Ramos to keep on looking. Within minutes another figure strode past the window. A man with thick, brown wavy hair and distinctive blue eyes. The man Adrian had come in search of.

Mark Farro.

Twenty-Six

AN HOUR LATER, Ramos held his position by the garden arch as the three white FBI vans he'd called in rolled to a stop outside Mark's cabin. Within seconds, agents poured out and stormed across the long yard. Some circled to the back of the cabin, while others went straight to the front door carrying a black metal battering ram.

The timber splintered and burst after just a few strikes. One agent called for any inhabitants to come out with their hands high and visible. For long seconds no one replied.

Guns drawn, the agent in command raised a hand, and some personnel behind him advanced into the building. Meanwhile, another agent stood yards away from Ramos, a crew of even more agents nearby like a second battalion ready to back up the first. Shouts came from inside the house, though no shots were fired. A suspenseful few seconds passed before an announcement cut through a radio that two people had surrendered and the investigative team could start rolling in.

The lead agent moved the remainder of his team in, but not before acknowledging Ramos with a nod to go in too. Even before Ramos got inside the cabin, a closer look through the front window showed the small space crammed with FBI. All areas of the property appeared swarmed with agents combing for evidence and information. Some cameras clicked, while others recorded video footage of the scene. Every drawer, every closet, every box had someone engaged in a search for further proof.

Occasionally, an agent filed out carrying a laptop or various piles of paper. Every so often, a bagged-up weapon would file past too. Handguns. Rifles. Knives. All brought here to protect Farro and his bodyguard, now just more things to incriminate him.

A solemn silence descended, and the sound of heavy footsteps had Ramos joining the vigil. The thunderous noise came from a short corridor adjoining the living room Ramos stood in. Farro's guard from the window earlier came out surrounded by several agents, his hands cuffed behind his back. Ramos stood aside to make some room, but the man's stare sought him as he called over the crush of people, "You'll vouch for me, right?"

The crush hurtled past, not allowing Ramos time to answer, though the guard twisted his head long enough for Adrian to offer a deep nod that when it came to any criminal trials, he would speak on this man's help in locating Farro.

After all, Adrian's brief time parading as a syndicate member had gifted him chances to befriend enough people there. Some not totally disagreeing with the part he'd played in Luciano Conti's arrest.

And yes, "befriend" was too strong a word. No one in the context of the syndicate were "friends." Not in an organization built on greed and taking advantage. Most people there were muscle for hire, hanging on for no other reason than to keep that machine running because they liked the money or couldn't escape. Chances were that Farro's bodyguard was far from the only man who wanted out. But examples such as the violent manhunt that unfolded after Dean Holloway's escape served as a cautionary tale of how little syndicate leaders cared about anyone's freedom.

Though Ramos never got close enough to make direct contact with Mark Farro, he'd still gathered leads and favor with those on the inside. He'd funneled information and incentives through his syndicate connections. Drawn closer and closer to those protecting Mark, enough to home in on this cabin in rural North Dakota.

Tonight's arrest was a major step forward, but still, Harlow couldn't breathe easy. Not until he ascertained the syndicate's next move. Whether they would finally back off now that Mark and his vendetta had nowhere to go.

The room's concentrated silence lingered with the muffled stomp of new footsteps against the carpet. Another small entourage flanked a handcuffed Mark Farro, his icy gaze quick to find Ramos.

"What good is being clever, Mr. Ramos"—a small smirk pulled his lips higher, and his stare took on an even deeper chill—"when you're in the wrong place?"

Not wanting to provide Farro the joy of any reaction, Ramos paused to process those words. What did he mean by *'in the wrong place'*?

None of today would have been possible without Adrian's months of work. Without his syndicate connections. Without their help, Mark Farro would never have been arrested. He frowned at the apathy in Mark's bold statement. At his lack of anger at his arrest. Like he'd wanted Ramos to be here.

Mark must have read the confusion in Adrian's frozen response because his smirk turned to an outright sneer. Even as the agents pulled him past, he did not look away. Though he did call out in a roaring laugh.

"You're too late. You're all far, far too late."

The early morning sky held a pale gray glow, the sun only just peeking over the mountainous horizon, as Laila steered her car closer to Harlow. Towering pine trees flicked past her window on the near-empty highway and provided space for her mind to wander. As tumultuous as things had been lately, she still had a lot to look forward to. Her summer classes would be finished soon, and she'd have some weeks off without study. She could have more time with Whitney, perhaps even Ramos would stick around. Because she *did* want him to stick around. But whether he could—or would—remained to be seen.

And on the topic of Ramos, she owed him a serious talk when she returned to town. She would lay out how she felt about her ex-husband's secret life and secret family. She'd share *all* her emotions. The anger. The betrayal. The fear. Her devastation on Whitney's behalf. That she'd have to one day sit her daughter down and tell her the horrid truth of Mike's choices.

Expressing her insecurities to Ramos would not be easy, especially when she also wanted to talk about how the secrecy around his work tweaked her insecurities. That watching his cold change during the showdown with Gerry had shocked and unsettled her.

She guided her car left and off the highway, higher and higher up a hill where a view of Harlow would soon open at the peak. A good portion of the town nestled snug between the region's rolling hills and she knew this path well. The lush golden wheat fields. The subdued light over the valley at this time of morning. She knew this place well enough that she could notice any differences immediately. Like now, as Harlow unfolded before her, and a litany of things appeared that *shouldn't* have been there.

The muddy gray sky. The columns of smoke dotting the valley. Her gut jolted with a wave of nausea. An icy chill filled her veins.

Harlow was on fire.

All of Harlow was on fire.

Instinct had her foot clamping down on the accelerator, as did the ingrained knowledge that summer's heat would make quelling the flames near impossible. And the worst of it... Somewhere amongst it all was Whitney.

Without her mother.

Scared.

And Laila still nowhere near enough to help.

Her throat swelled and formed a panicked sob, and she fought back tears, only for her thoughts to catch on Ramos. Just for this moment, she had to be more like him. *Run toward the danger. Not from it.* Her daughter needed her.

She swallowed at the tension in her throat and spoke out to her phone's voice command, the phone itself clipped to her windshield. "Call Mom."

The dial tone rang twice before her mother answered, her voice through the speaker a jumble of background noise and fraught words. "Laila, something terrible's happened."

"Is Whitney okay?" As much as a new sob worked up Laila's throat, she had to know her daughter was okay.

"Yes. Yes, she's fine, but the town's on fire." Her mom spoke quickly. "Where are you?"

"I know about the town, Mom, I'm on the mountain and can see it all." She peered to her left, where an influx of outbound traffic strained to escape in the opposite direction. "There's a lot of cars leaving, are you one of them?"

"No, Honey. There's too many of people fleeing, and they don't want a bottleneck of cars at every exit where people can get trapped in their cars. Our section of town isn't so bad yet, we've been told to gather in the town hall, but I'm not sure how long even this plan will hold."

Whitney's little voice came through all the background noise and Laila fought with herself to not exceed the speed limit more than she already did. Drawing closer to town, the fires grew increasingly visible, the pristine landscape littered with beacons of destruction, the morning light now holding an orange glow.

"I gotta go, Mom." The town's roadblock sat up ahead and she'd need to speak with the people there. "I'll see you soon."

With all the fires, getting to town hall wouldn't be straightforward, she hung up from her mother knowing she'd given a promise grounded in uncertainty.

Her stomach churned, as she pulled up to the line at the roadblock and tried to remain calm. The officer on duty leaned into the window of the car ahead, his finger pointed in the opposite direction to town. He stepped back, and the car proceeded to do as told and turned around.

She inched her car forward, knowing full-well that turning around would not be an option. Not for her.

The officer leaned in just as he had the car prior. "Morning, Miss."

"Officer, I live in Harlow." She attempted an affable smile, but the ache in her cheeks and the wobble of her lower lip said she failed. "My parents are down there with my daughter. I need to get through."

"I'm sorry, Miss." The man, perhaps somewhere in his early fifties, gave a sympathetic looking grimace that deepened the wrinkles over his cheekbones. "We can't let anyone in."

A sharp ache filled Laila's chest while she shook her head furiously, pulling her attention from the man standing between her and her child, and onto the two others patrolling the roadblock. They held an air of palpable unease, their wide gazes darting about and their movements stiff.

"I'm not turning around." Her voice rose a little and she turned back to the man peering through her window.

"Miss, I'm sorry." He held a calm tone and shook his head, his stoicism in what was a major crisis for her only working to agitate the panic gripping her every thought and feeling.

"I have to get in." She broke into an uncontrolled yell now and fresh tears burned down her cheeks. "Please. Just let me in."

"Ma'am." The officer's firm tone held an unmistakably assertive edge. "I'm going to have to ask you to settle dow—"

"No!" She slammed her hands into her steering wheel and lurched her car forward, refusing to be sidelined while her child was surrounded in flames.

The men around her broke into a flurry of movement, yelling indiscernible orders to each other, before the one she'd yelled at caught up to her car and wrenched her door wide open.

Even without him there, the metal barriers blocking the road meant her car *would* get stuck, nor would these men be so accommodating as to move those barriers out of her way.

In her agitated state, she jerked the handbrake into place, but kept the engine running. She launched out of her car and charged ahead, her breaths exploding with every hurried step. *She would move those damn barriers herself.* Then get in her car. Then get Whitney.

But of course, she had three grown men to fight first. So, before she got that far, three torsos caged her in, multiple arms locking around her.

"Let me go!" Her voice tore from her in a ragged and pain-filled cry, and she fought with every bit of energy she could muster, pushing forward despite the odds against her.

Her worst nightmare had come true. Whitney needed her, but she wasn't there, and these men weren't letting her correct her mistake. She had to get to Whitney. She just had to.

"Let me through." She kicked and shrieked but was being pushed in the opposite direction to where she sought to be. "Just let me through." Her back hit the side of her car and exhaustion and despondency drew the last dregs of will from her body. "I can't stay here while my daughter burns."

Twenty-Seven

RAMOS TOOK the highway back to Harlow, the speedometer on his car hovering just a few miles per hour above the limit. His thoughts refused to budge from what had just happened at Mark Farro's arrest, more precisely Mark's cryptic last warning, *"You're too late."*

Too late for what?

His heartbeat continued to race. The pieces of this puzzle just didn't make any sense. His instincts told him he would have his answers when he got back to Harlow. His fear was that he approached a whole other nightmare unto itself.

This is why I avoid getting too attached…

Mark hadn't seemed fazed with his arrest. Perhaps he was just playing it cool. A man incapable of believing anything bad could stick. But Ramos based that idea on pure assumption and had to be open to other possibilities. Like the syndicate and his connections having played him…

Or that Mark had planned on getting arrested all along.

But why?

He turned off the highway and up the hill, the engine revving against the incline and his mind sifting through what motivated a man like Mark Farro. Money and power were the obvious bet. And Ramos had spent enough time with career criminals to know most didn't want to waste their lives hustling.

They craved something more. Something hugely elusive when it came to organized crime. *Independence*. Especially the cold and calculated types, like Farro. He would never settle on a lifetime stint as Rudolph Manzinni's underling.

Ramos knew from his experience saving Dean's ass, that leaving an organization like the syndicate wasn't straightforward. One couldn't simply turn in their resignation letter and leave. The only exit options were death or prison.

Oh, shit! Prison.

Was prison Mark's plan?

Had he used his men and Ramos to get there?

Prison was a place he could shelter under the illusion that he'd taken a fall for the syndicate. He'd do his time. The syndicate wouldn't hurt him. Tonight's arrest would be his last grasp at freedom before he eventually moved on with his life.

Only one flaw impinged on that plan. That the syndicate would forgive Mark's failure to take revenge on Dean, Emilia, Chip, and all of Harlow.

A sick, skittery feeling burrowed deep within his gut. Like agitated bugs crawling through his insides. The revenge piece of this puzzle perhaps wasn't missing after all.

"You're too late."

Ramos pressed his foot harder to the accelerator, his nerves stripped raw from the hope he wasn't too late for anything. But as the car climbed the hill, opaque smoke from several fires devoured the spaces in and around Harlow.

Mark hadn't lied. Adrian *was* too late.

The roadblock ahead forced him to stop, the cars seeking entry into town backed up in front of him. A ragged female scream pulled at him from about six cars ahead. He rolled his window down, craning his neck for a better view.

There she stood, Laila, struggling against three officers. His heart sank at the grief written all over her face and fraught actions. He'd always thought himself a confident guy. Someone exceptionally good at what he did. But he'd fucked this up royally. Even if he'd had no idea of Mark's plans. Even if he couldn't be in two places at once. He'd played a role and would never forgive himself for the tragedy so quickly unfolding before him.

He launched out of his car and ran to help her, scrambling to make things right, shouting at the officers to let her go.

By now they had her pinned to her car and his shouts mingled with her wild cries. She twisted in the officer's hold, her cheeks red and wet, and her eyes wide but swollen, as her gaze caught on his.

"Help! Help me!" Her voice tore from her on a raw scream, somehow both a demand and a plea. "They won't let me get to Whitney!"

"Sir, step back. We have orders to stop anyone entering the valley." An officer held his hand up, creating a barrier between Ramos and her. A barrier he refused to accept.

"Officer, the fire below is likely the work of the syndicate." Though his warring emotions were anything but reasonable, he didn't draw closer and kept his tone even and firm. "My name is Adrian Ramos. You can call Sheriff Marlin and verify that I am part of the investigation into the syndicate. I intend to get into that valley, and I will be taking this woman with me."

Though the officer glared at him, not totally convinced or happy with Ramos pulling rank, all Ramos could think of was Mark's warning. That he *was* too late. But even as Harlow burned, with every fiber of his being, he didn't *want* to be too late. If anything happened to Whitney. All because he'd fallen into Mark's trap.

His attention fell to Laila again, her eyes glistening, while tears streaked her face and she muttered, "She's in there. She's in there."

And she was right. Whitney was in Harlow, and he didn't have time to waste. So, he stared down the officer ahead of him, uncertain what this man would say, only that, some way, somehow, he would get past this roadblock. "I assure you, Officer. I'll take all responsibility for what happens next."

The officer's expression hardened into an analytical scowl, like he didn't want to believe Ramos or do as asked. But something in the way Ramos spoke seemed to convey the fact that he could not be stopped.

That for once, following orders and taking all precautions wouldn't apply.

The officer grumbled something under his breath and stepped back, ordering the others to do the same. Adrian jumped into Laila's car and drove it out of the way and into an embankment. Before too long, she sat beside him in his car, and they embarked on the mad dash toward the raging fire.

Adrian's car roared down the road and Laila's chest heaved with a new wave of choking sobs. The air outside already thickened with smoke, mingling with the dust the car's tires churned through the rearview mirror. Meanwhile, an eerie silence hung between them, adding to the weight of panic pressing on her chest.

Ramos also kept casting sideways glances her way. Though she appreciated him helping her get past the roadblock, she could feel him analyzing her vulnerability through every stare. She didn't want his concern. *All she wanted was to find her daughter.*

Knuckles sore, she broke her tight hold on the armrest and leaned closer to the window. Deeper in the woods, plumes of curling smoke snaked through the trees, while her distorted image on the glass reflected back her tear-stained and bedraggled face.

"We'll get to her in time." Adrian's voice sent cold shock through her, as did the warmth of his hand as it came to rest on hers. That touch nearly burned her skin in contrast with where her mind went.

All the things that she could have done differently.

All the things that could still go wrong.

Feeling undeserving of any comfort, she snatched her hand back. "You don't know that for sure."

She didn't want any words of hollow hope.

This could get worse. This could get so, so much worse.

I could lose my daughter. Could lose Whitney.

His hand returned to the steering wheel in an act of seeming resignation, the shuttered look on his face mirroring her assessment of what went on in his head. "No, I don't. But I promised you we'd try out darndest, remember?"

She scoffed in a broken laugh and jutted her chin to the road, new tears spilling free. "That's my daughter down there. She dies, Ramos, then I... Failure isn't an option."

Though she couldn't finish her thoughts on what she'd do if anything happened to Whitney, his silence acknowledged what she'd meant. That she didn't want to exist in a world without Whitney. Especially if her absence coincided with her child's moment of need.

The lower they got into the valley, the smokier it got, until flames flickered into view farther down the road.

"Seems we'll have to improvise a way in." Adrian's tone sounded strong enough, but she caught the slight hesitation in his delivery. Like he too respected that fires had ways of diverting even the best plans.

A direct route to town was out of the question, so he slowed and took a counter-intuitive turn right.

She slammed her eyes shut and held back another wave of grief. "This won't ever end, will it?"

Hope drained from her with each passing second Ramos didn't answer. As though he didn't *need* to answer because his silence said everything. A silence that spoke of uncertainty. An inescapable situation that no amount of resilience could fix because Harlow was burning. *Literally burning.*

That crush of reality was too much to carry and her will faded with each smoke-tinged inhalation. Even if they survived today, life would never return to what it once was. Nor would Harlow. And the syndicate might *never* leave them be.

She peered out her window again and did her best to stay quiet. To let Ramos focus on getting them into town. Maybe Harlow did burn, but she was also saying goodbye, while bracing herself for what the unfolding hours would bring.

Burn it all. Just let Whitney escape safe.

A single tear rolled down her cheek and a sense of apathy made the scene outside somehow tolerable. Even as the next road brought flames lapping from the adjoining field, the air dry and haunting.

Still, we aren't all that far from town.

"Laila." Adrian reached for her again, and in her numb state, she let him. "I know we haven't been so close lately, but everything I do today will be about getting you and Whitney away from all this. Do you understand?"

Not wanting to speak for fear of what she'd say, she squeezed his hand, giving him the reaction he wanted. How could she explain that her trust in everything had become as charred as the fields outside? She would trust him in that she had little other choice, but nothing right now felt certain. Not even her opinions of the man beside her.

She'd seen him become someone else around Gerry Gibbons. His work had involved interacting with the syndicate. How else could she feel?

They reached two roads that led into town, one blocked off by walls of fire, the other the only viable option, though how long that would remain the case was anyone's guess. Not long, that was for sure.

He steered down the obvious path, where a house farther across a field stood engulfed in flames, that house belonging to Emilia and Blaine. Laila's tummy tensed at that sight. Another bad omen on her journey to get back to Whitney. As too were the emergency vehicles stationed along this road in an attempt to defend it.

Long minutes passed on that straight stretch of road until they finally reached the town's center, rounding another street, before they came to the town hall.

The moment the car stopped, she stumbled out her door, not even waiting for him to kill the engine, as she sprinted away, her heart pounding and her tight breaths burning her chest.

Everywhere she looked, the homes and businesses she'd known since childhood smoldered in ruins. Now, all she wanted was the familiarity of having her child in her arms. Of knowing Whitney was safe. Of having some semblance of comfort and control. Along with the illusion that she'd somehow get them out of here alive.

Twenty-Eight

LAILA BARGED through the town hall's large wooden doors, her gaze darting over the sea of faces holding expressions in various states of alarm. She proceeded to push through the crowd in search of her daughter, slow to succeed at that task, which forced her to pause and steady herself.

Drowning in the onslaught of worried murmurs around her and blinking away tears, she lashed her head from side to side. Still searching. Now sensing Ramos behind her, while she refused to look back at him.

Just keep looking forward. Find her. I have to find her.

Whitney's familiar swarthy features peeked through a gap in the crowd. A relieved sob broke from Laila, and she rushed forward, fighting against her overwrought emotions. She didn't want to scare her child more than she likely already was. But fighting any reaction became impossible as she pulled Whitney from her grandmother's arms and crushed the child's spindly body to her chest.

Suddenly, the soft tickle of those dark curls to Laila's cheek meant everything. It sparked a compulsion to ignore all warnings and turn and run from this awful dystopian scene.

"Thank you." She sniffed and addressed her mom from over

Whitney's shoulder. *Bless that woman. Bless her for so many things and in ways Laila could never hope to repay.* "Thank you for keeping Whit safe."

Her mother's lips pressed into a tight line, as though she fought back her own overwhelmed reaction, the wrinkles over her cheekbones deep and denoting a wariness Laila had never seen on her before.

"Where are all the others?" Laila asked the question because she wanted to know, but also to give her mother something new to focus on.

"Ally and Chip got out since the fire was closer to their side of town. But Dean and Sarah, Blaine and Emilia are all around here somewhere." Her mother peered about her, the action seeming rooted in the need for distraction more than anything else.

Laila mirrored her mother's movements. The new focus on everyone gathered lit a disconcerting idea. If the syndicate hoped to herd the people of this town to a select few spots, these fires succeeded. A glance over her shoulder to the sheriff seemed to validate the doubt taking up space in her stomach.

While Whitney remained in her arms, she turned and ventured toward the sheriff standing at the exit, brushing past Ramos and continuing to block him out. As much as she wanted to go, she had to pause as Emilia and Blaine approached.

"You got through the roadblock?" Emilia's eyes held a sad sort of joy, like, despite the miserable circumstance, she was genuinely glad to see Laila okay. "Did you happen to drive past our house? The fires were so close by the time we left, I was hoping, maybe—"

She didn't finish speaking before Blaine raised a hand and went to rubbing her back, the gesture seeming somewhat consoling, as though he'd come to terms with a sobering reality that she still held hope over.

Laila's heart strained, but she'd spent years learning to do difficult jobs, and so she didn't seek to draw out Emilia's pain with denial. She gave a slow shake of her head and whispered a weak, "I'm sorry."

Emilia's lips wobbled and water gathered in her eyes, but she offered a grateful nod all the same. This woman had already lost one home to flames and the syndicate, and here she stood, life still in danger and her home gone. Laila wanted to stay and comfort Emilia, but she had other priorities right now, while Blaine stood by ready to help his new wife.

So, she dropped her gaze and avoided any more talk, pushing past and proceeding onto the sheriff, the man still half a hall away. Squeezing through a throng of people wasn't easy. A number of those gathered lifted their heads, lips parting as though they sought to stop and talk to her. But she simply shook her head at them and continued to move on.

The sheriff spotted her approach just before she stopped before him, her voice wavering as she spoke. "Can I leave?"

She already sensed what the answer would be.

The sheriff eyed her, but his focus soon stopped on Whitney, a momentary look of remorse cracking his stony expression, as he shook his head. "The roads are backed up as it is, and I wouldn't advise it. You could get trapped. If you can hold on for a little longer, we'll have new routes cleared and two lanes of traffic open on a designated safe route out. We'll also have a crew to guide the way."

Laila bit down an instinctive need to protest and glanced behind her at the mass of people, with their faces pale in clear distress. Much of this lot would have witnessed the flames outside too. They'd be just as desperate to leave. But the sheriff was right. There could be safety or pandemonium in numbers. With her and Adrian's wild ride in, at least the new lanes would have emergency crew to keep the peace.

And still, looking around, this place felt less like a community hall and more like the inside of a sinking passenger ship—everyone simply waiting for the moment to collectively drown.

That thought turned her tummy rock hard, but she nodded in a solemn promise to the sheriff that she would stay put. At least for now.

Just then, the doors to the sheriff's left burst open and Ted Boseman, a local farmer, crashed through. He shoved at an unfamiliar man, pushing the guy, while holding his hands together behind his back, and yelling out for everyone to hear.

"Caught this one crossing my field on foot and a gasoline can in hand." He gave the man one final hard nudge toward the sheriff, the sheriff extending his hands to catch him. Dean Holloway stepped up to help, the sheriff already inundated with a constant stream of updates crackling over his radio.

Dean ushered the apprehended man to an empty chair by the entry wall, accepting a pair of the sheriff's handcuffs in the process.

The sheriff finished responding to the comms on his radio, then clapped Ted on the back. "Great job there, Ted. Sorry to say, he's not the first one we've caught this morning. This was clearly an organized attack, and as much as I'm sure Dean could shake the truth out of that one, I doubt he'd tell us anything we haven't already guessed for ourselves."

"It's the damn syndicate, isn't it?" Ted held a gruff tone, his dirt-stained hands curled into fists at his sides as if he truly wished to hit someone.

The sheriff nodded. "Ramos helped apprehend Mark Farro just this morning. Seems the arrest came hours too late."

Laila's jaw dropped open, and she spun around to find Ramos still behind her, his cheeks sunken like he understood exactly what thoughts ran through her head. *He hadn't told her.* Hadn't even given a clue of what he would be doing last night. He hadn't even mentioned Mark Farro's name. Much less that he'd planned his arrest.

The sheriff knows more about this man than I do.

To make matters worse, Gerry Gibbons squeezed in on the conversation, his wife and three kids only yards away. And of course, Lenny Brooks stood even closer.

"So, what you're saying is that this won't all end with Mark Farro?" Gerry held a scrunched expression, as though he'd already forgotten all about Laila kicking his ass and that Ramos hadn't been far off joining her. "Is that right?"

"There are no guarantees." The sheriff shrugged, a new level of wariness shadowing his face. "But we have another key syndicate member off the street, and that's something."

"Still not enough." Gerry scoffed and turned his scowl to Laila. Maybe the ass-kicking wasn't so forgotten. "Someone'll replace him, just like how he took over from Luciano Conti. Rudolph Manzinni is still out there too. No one knows what he looks like *or* where he is."

His words dripped in hate and venom, and he directed it all on

Laila, as if she embodied everything wrong with this day and all the events that led up to it. His cold delivery had her clinging tighter to Whitney, seeking comfort, while offering protection.

"You lot shoulda moved on when we said." Lenny drew in closer now, his tight movements holding just as much malice. "Now there's no more Harlow for you or us."

Though she couldn't understand why they took this all out on her, it seemed her close physical proximity made for reason enough. Lenny took another step toward her, and she inched back. Surely he wouldn't hurt a woman with a small child in her arms.

"Mommy, I want to go." Whitney's tinny tone mirrored Laila's fear, and she sought to fulfill her daughter's wishes, only for Ramos to step out in front of her.

"Why don't you address those sentiments to me or Mr. Holloway?" He used his body to block any attacks, as well as Laila's view. "Instead of trying to scare a woman and her child?"

"What do you care?" This time Gerry piped up, and she saw past Ramos enough to catch Gerry lifting his chin in defiance. "You'll be kickin' off soon enough, won't you? While we'll be the ones dealing with a burnt-out town. You got no place interfering."

Ramos didn't so much as move, though Laila figured she was best to get out from behind him should a real fight break out. She stepped to the side and increased her distance from the men, where she also had a better view of what went on.

"I have every reason to care what happens here today." Though his words hinted at his feelings for Laila, the disconcerting iciness from that first run-in with Gerry was back on his face. "Back up, now. Go join your family."

Gerry's face went red, and he did the opposite of what he was asked, puffing his chest out and taking up more space. "You telling me what to do again?"

"Sure." Despite the sarcasm, Adrian gave nothing away. "It worked out so well for you last time. Now, run along."

Gerry's face turned all red and angry, a hint of shame perhaps adding to his color. He was a high school bully not used to being bullied. Conditions such as these held the potential to erupt in unpredictable ways. "You lot have ruined everything. We're all gonna die. You think I give a shit about doing what you say?"

He made a hocking sound and then spat at Adrian's feet. All chatter in the hall died instantly. Again, Adrian didn't react, which only added to the weighty anticipation in the air. And then, Gerry, in all his impulsive stupidity, lunged forward and shoved Ramos hard in the chest.

Ramos held his ground but put a hand out to create more distance. Gerry flinched, seeming to misinterpret the move as an attempted strike, and swung a fist out at Ramos.

His blow connected with Adrian's right cheek. Laila gasped and shielded Whitney's eyes from whatever happened next. Meanwhile, to her right, Gerry's wife screamed. His kids were quick to start sobbing. Lenny, on the other hand, looked pale and inched back into the crowd. All bluster and no action. And Laila's attention caught on an uncharacteristically gray-faced Rochelle nearby.

"That's enough, Gibbons!" Sheriff Marlin bellowed out and came up to Gerry, wrenching his arms behind him and hauling him away from Ramos. "If not for the fire, I'd have you locked in a cell."

"We have nothing left." Even as the sheriff dragged Gerry toward the door, he struggled and shouted, the red anger in his eyes now verging on tears.

The crowd's stunned silence continued, and Gerry's hostility hung like a prickling heat in the air. That heat turned her thoughts to her visions of the town on fire. To Emilia's face upon learning her house was gone. To the multitude of familiar faces around her holding unfamiliar looks of despair.

Maybe Gerry was right. Maybe anyone remotely linked to the syndicate should have left. Maybe she was in part to blame.

"Don't you worry, Gerry." Lenny Brooks seemed to find his words again, as he pushed back out through the crowd, his face beet red while he stabbed a finger toward his friend. "We'll get 'em all back some way."

Her stomach dropped, his threat feeling like yet another bomb ready to explode. As if this town didn't have enough threats and real-world tragedy to worry about…

"Stop it. Just stop it!"

The usually even-keeled Rochelle jolted forward, her tone a frazzled shout as though she'd lost her very last bit of patience. "I thought this was a sweet little town full of equally charming people…"

She shook her head, making it clear she didn't think that way anymore.

"When will you all just stop attacking each other?" She ran her gaze over the feuding men, and across to Gerry's sobbing children, the pull of muscles over her face releasing to a slack sort of resignation. "If you want to hate anyone, then hate me. Just stop fighting, okay?"

Gordon stepped out and draped his arm around her shoulder, rubbing her upper arm as he dropped a soft kiss to her head. "No one here could ever hate you."

"Yes, they could." She gave a small, but shaky nod directed at the ground, and tears welled in her eyes. "And they *should* hate me."

Though the violent tension faded from the air, a heavy silence remained, the whole town listening to see what this woman would say next.

Rochelle's tears broke free and splashed down her perfectly made-up cheeks, and she lifted her gaze, seeming to address all the people staring at her. "You all should hate me because I'm Rudolph Manzinni."

Twenty~Nine

A SIMULTANEOUS GASP broke across the large room at town hall, before the rumble of murmurs spread like a slow tidal wave over the crowd. Adrian stared at Rochelle and struggled to make sense of what she'd just said. That *she* was Rudolph Manzinni.

A soft shuffling sound brought his attention to Emilia pushing through the stunned faces to his left, her cheeks hollow and eyes wide with shock.

"Rochelle?" She moved past him, her voice wavering on a breathy tone.

She'd known Rochelle far longer than anyone in this town. With her past run-ins with the syndicate, Rochelle's unlikely claim of being Rudolph Manzinni seemed extra cruel.

The pinch of Rochelle's face eased, and she lifted her hands in a gesture to the crowd, her eyes taking on a soft and heartbroken sheen. "There's a raging fire outside. Everyone is turning on each other... I just... I just never thought it would come to this."

Emilia stood before her friend and shook her head in a slow and seemingly unconscious motion, her eyes welling as she spoke again. "What are you saying? What have you done?"

"Nothing intentional." Rochelle took a quick step forward, but Emilia held a hand up and backed away.

A heavy pause lingered between the women where Blaine Callaghan came to his wife's side, his arm snaking around her waist in a protective hold.

Rochelle's gaze danced over the couple, and she held an open look of loneliness, even though she had her own man, Gordon, nearby. Still, she sucked in a shaky breath and nodded to herself, as though she accepted the gulf her statement put between this old friendship.

Next, she turned to Ramos, a more stoic look taking her over. "That night at Maynard's when you gathered everyone together to discuss the syndicate. I heard the name Rudolph Manzinni, and it sounded so familiar. Though I couldn't quite place it, something didn't feel right, and I had a moment of panic. That's when you questioned me and I kind of—"

"Got defensive?" Ramos frowned, and she nodded her consensus. Next, his thoughts shifted to that day when she'd come to find him at Laila's doorstep. Only, the fire at the Coopers' store interrupted whatever she'd stopped by to say.

He narrowed his stare at her, frown deepening because—even though he still couldn't quite see this innocuous woman as a mafia boss—it appeared he had missed some kind of big opportunity all those weeks ago. "You tried to tell me, didn't you?"

She nodded. "But then I saw what the syndicate did to the general store, and I chickened out. Everyone was so scared and so much damage had already been done. I felt so guilty and concerned for my own safety, I just kinda locked up and couldn't find a way to share what I know."

"Why are you all standing there doing nothing?" Lenny Brooks shouted from behind Dean, keeping back as though he knew not to get too close. "Why don't you tackle the bitch like you just did Gerry?"

The crowd's low rumble grew in volume. Confusion, panic, and anger converged into one. Rochelle was right about one thing. These people *were* turning and something needed to be done to keep everyone safe.

"Is there a separate room somewhere so we can question her?" He directed the question to the sheriff, not wanting to risk Rochelle blurting out more sensitive information in front of this whole town. Or worse, someone hurting her before she got the chance to explain.

The sheriff nodded to the door. "Just down the hall. I'll come with you."

Ramos took hold of Rochelle's arm and tugged her along, addressing Dean and Blaine as he strode out. "Can you two keep an eye on everyone in here?"

"Sure thing. We'll find you if we need you." Though Dean spoke, Ramos turned his focus over his shoulder to Laila clutching Whitney in her arms. He sent her a look of reassurance, despite his stomach churning with unquenchable doubt.

Down the wide hallway was a small office, and the sheriff shut the door behind them as the trio entered, the room cramped, while Rochelle held her silence.

"Explain." Ramos forced an even tone and maintained his stillness, not wanting to scare her into saying nothing. Even if he did need her to hurry up and cut to the truth. Slowing down often had the counterintuitive effect of speeding some things up.

Rochelle peered up at him through a pained grimace, her arms wrapped around her waist and highlighting the expensive soft looking fabric to her sapphire blue t-shirt. "My grandfather died when I was twelve years old, but he left a whole lot of money to me for when I turned eighteen. Way more money than any one person, much less a teen, should own. I had dreams beyond joining LA's social set, so before I embarked on my life of travel and furniture dealing, I hired a lawyer to manage my affairs. I asked that a good portion of my inheritance be invested in a way that would benefit the charities I'd chosen, and that I not receive any attention for any large donations. I wanted it all to remain a secret. I didn't want any extra attention that might get in the way of me enjoying my freedom."

She paused and tugged the long strap of her ice-blue purse higher onto her shoulder, her eye line connecting with the sheriff leaned against a desk in the far corner. "My lawyer did a bunch of stuff to make all this happen. He set up an LLC, applied for an assumed name certificate, set himself up as a go-between agent. Honestly, I can't recall every detail, only that every transaction would always point back to one fake name. *Rudolph Manzinni.*"

Instant coldness hit his core and Adrian's shoulders sank with a sudden sense of doom. Her recent outburst made a whole lot more sense now. As did her story—since she and Emilia were from the same circles—and the syndicate had first followed Emilia to this town. "I take it all this happened about eleven years ago?"

That's when the syndicate first appeared. Starting with small crimes and working and recruiting their way up from there.

Rochelle pressed her lips together and nodded. "I had no idea. Honestly, I didn't. My balances looked about right, but I didn't really dig all that deeply. I just assumed everything money related was being looked after as requested."

Her gaze dropped again, as did her expression, her slumped stance denoting shame. Within three years of access to her money, the syndicate had grown to having cells in most major cities across America.

Hinting he wanted to say something, the sheriff pushed away from the desk. "So, just to be clear, all this time you thought you were funding a bunch of charities?"

"And instead, I was bank-rolling a crime ring." A tight and manic laugh broke from her, before water splashed down her cheeks on a heavy rain of tears and she clapped a hand over her mouth, as though wracked with a new wave of quilt. "People lost their homes today. Oh, God. And how many have died over the years at the hands of the syndicate? And it's my fault. It's all my fault."

He strode closer and pressed a hand to her shoulder, believing her story about being clueless this whole time. "You were young when this all started, and you trusted that the people you paid to manage your affairs would do their job. You made an innocent mistake."

"No, but I should have known." She held a hand out, signaling she didn't want his offer of comfort, that perhaps she didn't believe herself worthy of it. "So much for everything my grandfather built. So much for my family's dreams of setting a good example for our community. So much for freedom, I'm going to prison."

Looking truly broken, she dipped her head and buried her face in her hands. If she didn't want him to comfort her, then maybe she'd accept something a little more proactive.

"Something that might go a long way to avoiding that would be doing everything possible to help us track down the people behind all this."

He caught the sheriff's eye and the man nodded, before joining in the attempt to reason with Rochelle. "Miss Ferrara, if you want to be more than a naive girl who trusted the wrong man with your money, you might start by telling us who this lawyer of yours is?"

She huffed out a soft laugh and shook her head. "You're going to think this is even more ridiculous."

"Tell us anyway." Ramos sent her a soft glare, one that said there wasn't anything she could say that would be considered ridiculous if it led to this whole fiasco being over.

She held his stare for a few beats, a new stillness entering her demeanor. "Okay, fine. It's Enzo Costa."

He suppressed an instant urge to groan and instead pinched the bridge of his nose, glancing over at the sheriff, who held a stupefied gape of his own. "Let me get this straight, you transferred the power over your money to Enzo Costa? The hokey celebrity lawyer with failed aspirations of a political career?"

"Because he's a complete tool, right?" She rolled her eyes but shook her head. "Except, he was still an up-and-comer a decade ago. Someone well-regarded in our community at the time. His 'tooliness' was much more covert. Like you said, I didn't know any better and I simply went with the guy everyone else trusted. My biggest failing is that I never really thought much of it thereafter." She shrugged, looking a little hopeless. "Even if he did become less than what I expected, by the time that happened, he owned a large law firm and I figured he probably wasn't even the one running the financial side of things anymore."

Though Ramos tried to remain non-judgmental, he couldn't help but say, "That's a whole lot of assumptions."

"I know." She looked down at the ground and sighed. "I should have stayed on top of things, but I was busy on my adventures. Hindsight is a hell of a thing."

She peered up at the sheriff just as his radio blared with a new update. He disconnected from the conversation to answer. Apparently, the roads were now open in two lanes as promised and the time had come to evacuate the town hall. As much as everyone here would leave, he and the sheriff still had obligations that would keep them from tending to any personal dilemmas.

Not wanting to waste any more time, he hooked his arm around Rochelle's elbow and guided her out the door, staying with her by the main hall, while the sheriff met with Blaine and Dean just inside. "Enlist all the help you can to clear this building. Start with the Coopers. I saw them around here somewhere. Most people will respect whatever orders they pass on."

"Sure thing." Dean patted the sheriff's back, before the sheriff turned back to Ramos, taking Rochelle's arm. "Go settle things with Laila. I've got this one for now."

He nodded his thanks and found Laila not far from where he'd left her at the top of this crowd. Her parents were close by now and Whitney held her grandma's hand. So, he took Laila a little farther away, demanding her full attention. "Listen, I have calls to make and can't leave yet, but you and Whitney go with your parents. Don't stick around here. Got it?"

Her eyelids flared wide, and her gaze fluttered about his face, like she read the unspoken message in his words. That he didn't fully know what would happen next or when he would see her again.

"You won't stay back long?" The strain across her face turned slack with understanding and her voice trembled. "Will you?"

He shook his head, wanting to tell her not to worry, but knowing everything about this situation warranted concern. "Only for the urgent stuff. The sheriff is taking Rochelle and I'll do what I can on the road on my way out of town." He took hold of her cheeks, and as much as she'd wanted to keep their relationship a secret, he couldn't deny himself one final and desperate kiss. "Listen to me, the syndicate will know I played a part in Mark Farro's arrest. They'll be looking for me, so I need to stay clear of you and Whitney until this is all over. Do you remember your promise to me?"

She began to shake her head as if she didn't want to accept what he asked, only to pause and for a wider look of understanding to take over. He asked her to keep the promise he'd had her make the night at the hospital. The one that, when the situation called for it, she would put herself and Whitney first.

That situation was now.

"For a number of reasons, it's best you and Whitney aren't with me." He ran a thumb over her cheek and her expression crumbled into a look of broken acceptance. "I can't message or call you, it's too risky. If I can, I'll try to get word to you some other way, but…"

His words trailed because there was no positive spin to this. There'd be no telling how long they'd be separated. Days. Maybe months. Perhaps he would never stop being a target. Either way, obstructing the syndicate signed the death warrant on this relationship, and once again, a man Laila cared for was leaving her.

Once again, he berated himself for getting involved. As if he could have ever controlled his emotions when it came to this woman. And still, she'd drawn him in. And he'd pursued her. That would likely always be his biggest mistake.

Had he caused her more trouble for simply knowing him?

Since this wasn't the time for finding out, he let her go, hoping against all hope that he'd soon settle the whole saga with Enzo Costa parading as Rudolph Manzinni. That Laila would be safe, and that, as much as her pleading eyes now begged him to come with her, she would stay safe and leave this burning town behind once and for all.

Thirty

ONE DAY AFTER HARLOW BURNED, Laila lay on a bunk in the crammed school gymnasium of the neighboring town of Marston. Whitney slept tucked under her arm. Partly because Whit hadn't wanted her own bunk. Partly because Laila wanted to keep her daughter close. And, of course, Laila couldn't sleep.

That said, she suspected she wasn't the only one having trouble closing her eyes. So many of her fellow Harlow residents surrounded her tonight. So many displaced. So many having lost so much. And just as when she'd had to move into Aggie's cottage, once again she was displaced, too. Forced to sleep in a bed that wasn't her own. Out of her element. Just counting down the minutes, like everyone else here, before she could return to town to see what was left of her former life.

From what she'd witnessed yesterday, there wouldn't be much.

And what about Ramos? The last she'd heard from the sheriff was that Adrian had returned to LA. Back to his job. But Adrian, himself, was yet to contact her.

Maybe he would never return to Harlow.

Maybe she couldn't blame him.

She wasn't so sure she wanted to go back either.

Her arm had turned numb from the weight of Whitney's head, so she shifted under the scratchy, moss green emergency blanket and rolled to her side. She kissed Whit's temple, finding some comfort in the softness of her child's skin. Meanwhile, her gaze caught on her mother staring back at her through the darkness. Her eyes were pinched, and her forehead scored in lines from the same worried look she'd sent Laila all throughout the day.

Worry seems to be a mother's default emotion.

Laila locked her arm tighter around Whitney. This situation was everything she *hadn't* wanted for her child. Perhaps the same thought ran through her mother's mind when she looked at Laila.

Heartbroken. Injured. Broke. Homeless.

Surely things can't get any worse?

Condensing all her problems like that made her eyes stung and her throat tighten. Not that she'd had any shortage of tears lately. She only let those fall when she got a moment away from Whitney.

She could have tonight. To feel sad. To feel a little hopeless. Before she'd do what she'd always done and find a way to dig them out of this pit. Even when she'd already thought the odds were impossible to overcome. Even when she'd already thought she had nothing.

There's always something more to lose. Isn't there?

She didn't know how to fix any of this, only that the guilt of Whitney having to endure so much upheaval spurred Laila away from feeling sorry for herself for too long. This would have to be her rock-bottom. Soon enough, she would pick herself up and get back to making the best of a sucky situation. Her dreams of a better life would come true.

Because some things couldn't be burned.

All the work she'd done so far. Her nearing graduation day. She still had those. And Ramos or not, her life would improve.

It had to.

Adrian hid in the shadows behind the bright lights and cameras at LA's new number one morning TV show, *The Wake-Up Call*. An apt name given Enzo Costa sat with the show's two hosts up ahead on a cozy blue couch, laughing and chatting through a commercial break, about to receive the biggest shake-up of his entire life.

After getting hold of Enzo's schedule, this window in his plans had been chosen as the ideal moment to bring him in. What was supposed to be a lighthearted guest political commentator spot, would soon become anything but.

But why here and why now? Because Enzo wouldn't be within the fortress of his home or office. He'd be in a public setting. On live TV. With less protection around him and without the advantage of his usual controlled environment. The show's producers had jumped on the idea. Drama, and a spike in tv rankings, in exchange for this calculated chance to take down Enzo Costa.

The commercial break ended, and Enzo used the remaining seconds before the cameras cut to him to straighten his blue-gray suit and run a hand over his dyed-brown hair. The older man seemed to also want to hide his years with an unnatural covering of brown fake tan. In the next beat, the male host began addressing the show's audience through the camera, and Adrian and the agents beside him readied to pounce.

The female host cut in now and ran through a short list of Enzo's achievements, before introducing him. Though she held an expected morning TV style exaggerated smile, her gaze flicked over to Adrian with the hint of a nervous grimace.

It had been decided that Adrian would be the public face of this arrest. The syndicate already knew about him. There would be less risk to anyone else involved.

But right now, he wanted to give Enzo a little more time to settle in. To feel sure about himself. He allowed the man to embark on a long explanation on his views on a local politician's campaign strategy, to make a joke that earned laughter from the hosts, that small high point seeming like a better opportunity for Adrian to interrupt. Just as Enzo's greed had interrupted and disturbed the lives of so many others.

"Excuse me, Mr. Costa," He kept his voice even and composed, stepping past the cameras. "We need you to come with us. Now."

Enzo stopped mid-sentence and his expression went slack with shock and confusion. Six agents lingered back, out of the camera's view, but ready to help Adrian at any moment. Even more agents filed in from two side-doors, outnumbering the few men Costa had brought for protection.

Enzo's gaze darted about, before he recovered with a forced smile and a chuckle of fake merriment. As though he sought to stall for his next move. Ever the lawyer. Ever the politician. Ever the criminal looking for a way out. "What is this all about?"

"I'm sure you know." Adrian shifted to a position behind the couch and hooked his fingers under Enzo's armpits, bringing his hands behind him and hoisting the man out of his seat. "And I'm sure you don't want me to list your alleged crimes here on live TV. So, it's best you come along now."

"I don't know what you're talking about." Enzo struggled and turned a pleading look to the hosts beside him, those two now clutching each other some yards from the couch.

But Enzo had a solid three decades on Ramos and his struggling and pleading couldn't stop the metallic click of Adrian's cuffs around his wrists—a sound that brought a genuine flutter to Adrian's heart—even if he didn't yet know whether this arrest would be enough. Whether he would be able to get back to his life with Laila. Or whether she would even want him back.

At least there's one less syndicate person on the streets. And the ringleader, at that.

Actually, more than one syndicate member. Because, at that exact moment, all the extra agents here to help Adrian unleashed a symphony of scuffles and more clicks of handcuffs, as each of Costa's men here also got arrested.

Amongst all the shouts and movement came another distinctive sound, the tap of high heels over the polished concrete. Rochelle stepped out from the fray behind the cameras. She clutched a burgundy purse and a slow and knowing smile, looking pristine as ever. "Does the name, Rochelle Ferrara, sound familiar?"

As much as Adrian had tried to stop her from being here, Rochelle had insisted, and the next few seconds made him a little glad she had.

Enzo's leathery cheeks turned instantly pale, and his eyes glazed over like he'd seen a ghost. And maybe, to some extent, that much was true. He'd figured Rochelle too rich and stupid to ever find out about Rudolph Manzinni's detour into crime. But here she was. Back from the past to haunt him.

Either way, he stopped struggling—and cameras still rolling—he didn't fight Adrian's next effort to move him on. His shoulders slumped and his step were shuffled, but he followed every directive on the way to the elevator.

Just like a man who understood that life as he knew it was over.

Thirty-One

LAILA KILLED the engine to her car, her eyelids heavy and her limbs aching from another overnight shift at the grocery store. The time on her dash said 7:10 am and, yet again, a pale morning light crested the roof of her house up ahead. One of the few houses to survive the fires three months ago.

As usual, she was exhausted and still had more books to crack open now that school was back. *Unlike* usual, her mother wouldn't be bringing Whitney by, because for the time being, Laila's parents lived with her while their house was being reconstructed.

The fires had claimed so much more than her parents' home. More than fifty percent of this town's houses and businesses had been extinguished with the flames, and Harlow was in the grips of a huge rebuild. There were never enough hands and resources to go around, but somehow, working together to overcome tragedy had the effect of dowsing months of prior unrest.

It didn't hurt that the syndicate had also left Harlow alone since then. As far as she knew, there was no syndicate anymore.

Not that she could know for sure. She hadn't spoken to Ramos in months, so had no insider knowledge, though her body and soul still ached every time he entered her mind.

She let out a sigh and braced to reenter the pandemonium of her home, but first she turned and opened her car door, only to pause at the sight of a car waiting in the driveway next door. A midnight blue SUV.

Adrian's car.

"No way." She stepped out onto her driveway, her voice breathy, while her mind grappled with the sight before her.

"I figured you'd be back 'round about this time."

She startled at the sound of his voice coming from behind her, then spun around to find him seated on her doorstep and clearly waiting for her.

A slow smile pulled at her lips and tears welled in her eyes. Her body worked off pure instinct and she raced toward him, arms outstretched and heart racing. He found his feet just in time to catch her in a desperate embrace.

His strong arms wrapped around her, and he pressed his lips to the top of her head.

"Adrian." She clung to him as if she were afraid he would fade away like a dream.

He kissed the top of her head again, but remained silent while he held her close. Meanwhile, she buried her face into the side of his neck and breathed him in. That familiar peppery cologne mixed with the salty musk of his skin.

"Now, this is the reception I hoped for." He chuckled and stepped back just far enough to look into her eyes and give her a gentle smile. "It's been too long."

Something about the reminder of the months and miles that had kept them apart hit her with a cold slap of reality. That, as much as she loved having him back, she couldn't be sure if his return was the best for everyone involved.

"It has been too long." She stepped back some more, straightening the hem of her scarlet work vest, the brown fall leaves scuttling along her drive yet another reminder of just how much time had passed.

She peered up to catch him frowning at her, like he caught the subtleties in her actions and words. His gaze softened and he reached for her. Despite her reservations, she allowed him to draw her closer.

"Seems we have a lot to talk about first."

She looked up and caught both sadness and hope reflected in his eyes, that hope spurring her to offer a small nod. "Still, feels so good to see you again. You look great on TV, by the way."

She smiled up at him, hoping he'd accept her small peace offering.

"You saw that, huh?"

"You mean, Enzo Costa's arrest? Who *hasn't* seen it?" She huffed out a chuckle. "If town hall hadn't burned down, I'm pretty sure the Coopers would have staged a town gathering to watch, complete with wide-screen projectors and shared plates."

"Maybe I should quit my current gig and find a new career on morning TV?"

"You, quit?" She scoffed and laughed all at once.

"Okay, well, maybe not a TV career. I'm not sure I'd be cut out for that kind of work, anyway. It's a bit too... shiny, but"—his hand clasped tighter around hers, and he seemed to vie for her full attention —"Harlow still needs a lot of help. I have two hands and my years in the service have given me some experience in post-disaster rebuilds. Besides, there's a woman I'd like to stay for." He shrugged as though his proposal was nothing, though the strain across his face said his bid to stay meant everything. "Maybe quitting isn't so farfetched."

"I don't know if I can ask you to do that." She pressed her lips together, instantly regretting what she'd said. Even if it was the truth. "And I don't know if I can trust myself to let you make such a huge life change. So much has happened, Ramos, and—"

"You need a moment to catch your breath?" One corner of his lip ticked upward, a little hurt, but understanding. "You and me both."

"I feel like we're only now getting back to basics." She shrugged and squeezed his hand. "There's no syndicate. No nasty letters on my doorstep. Jeeze Louise, I thought my life was complicated just raising Whitney alone. That'll teach me to complain."

In truth, she'd only recently come to release all the negativity of these last years. Of Mike leaving. Of having to shoulder so much alone. Of learning she and Whitney had been abandoned for another family. And she'd spent so much time focusing on all that was difficult, she'd been mostly blind to just how damn lucky she was. To have her child and her family. To even have the opportunity to study and reconstruct her life from the ground up.

"In so many ways, you're just like him." Her voice hitched at that surprise comparison to Mike, and Ramos flinched.

She'd held that thought so closed in her heart all this time, but now that he was here, she couldn't imagine talking about getting back together without dragging this out into the light too.

"I understand why." She shrugged again, but this time her movements were weaker, and her voice held a tinny and wounded edge. "You were just doing your job, but there were so many secrets. And then just as you started to make a home in my heart, you were gone." A tear rolled down her cheek and she dropped her gaze to his chest, because looking in his eyes hurt too damn much. "Just gone. Zero contact until now."

He said nothing and the silence eventually forced her to look back up at him, his face pale and hollow, like he cursed himself for leaving when and how he had. That he hadn't fully considered that his exit might have reopened old wounds.

"I didn't have any choice." His jaw wavered, as though he second-guessed that explanation. "I needed to keep you and Whitney safe—"

"I know. I know." Feeling a little ridiculous for making an issue out of this, she squeezed her eyes shut and shook her head. Ridiculous or not, she needed to say her piece. "I want to keep us safe too. And being safe doesn't just mean physically. There's trust, Ramos. Trusting you. Trusting that this is all over and things will finally be okay. There's trusting myself, because every decision I make is a decision I make for Whitney, too. And I don't have any trust in any of that right now. None."

Ramos held her gaze for the longest time, his cheeks straining and releasing as though he fought a silent war within himself, though his spare hand cradled hers in his. "I wished I had the right words..."

He grimaced and took his gaze away from her, shaking his head at the ground as though he berated himself for failing. "I want so much more for us."

Her heart clenched at that and the muscles in her throat swelled with a need to release the sob she kept buried deep within. "Yeah, me too."

His brow furrowed and he peered up at her through the downward tilt of his chin. "You know, I've spent my entire life avoiding getting too attached."

The tension across his brow melted into a soul-shattered and wide expression. "And then I go and do something truly moronic like getting attached to the one woman who really shouldn't have me in her life." He released a broken laugh—and to her utter shock—this unruffled man, with all his stoicism—had water gathering along the lower edges of his eyes. "I'm sorry for putting you in that position. Not only leaving, but fearing for your safety. You're right, I wasn't in the best place to ask for your trust, and then you trusted me anyway, and I'm hoping you'll come around to trusting me again."

"Adrian, it's okay—"

"I'm afraid, Laila." He paused and swallowed hard in the wake of a small crack in his voice, his firm tone a hint he wanted her comfort less than to have his say, just as she had. "I'm afraid because I don't love my job, but my job sure loves me. The truth is, I'm good at what I do, and my work saves lives. And while you and Whit showed me pieces of myself I didn't know existed, I'm scared that the lines of what I do and who I am have become blurred. That you might walk away today thinking that I loved my job any more than I loved you. When nothing could be further from the truth."

Everything within her paused.

To hear that he loved her.

That she hadn't been alone the entire time she'd been falling for him.

So rarely had she ever been stunned speechless, but this was one of those moments, and her mouth hung limp and open, while nothing but a raspy croak escaped.

Adrian is not like Mike.

Adrian came back.

New lines formed between his brows, his gaze shifting about her face as though he considered he might have said the very thing he shouldn't have, when he'd really just uttered the exact words she'd wanted to hear. Not only from him, but in all those years she'd been pushing through, just her and Whitney.

"I get that you have your own reasons for wanting to keep away, but don't let one of those reasons be that you think you're asking too much." He stepped closer, but then stopped as if he second-guessed the move. "You're not asking too much, Laila." He dropped to one knee, and she backed up, letting out a gasp. "Not when I'm begging you to ask for everything I have to offer."

She pressed her hands to her mouth and tears spilled down her cheek. "I'm really confused about what's happening right now. Is this a proposal?"

His expression sank and he peered about him and then down at himself, like he hadn't been all that conscious about falling to his knees. "I hadn't planned on that. I'm not even sure what I was thinking." He snapped his chin higher and caught her gaze, his brows squishing together. "But I'll say, 'Yes' if you say, 'Yes'."

She broke into laughter, and his lips broke into a slow and twisted smile, his steadfast stare holding a pleading sort of edge.

She reached out her hands and claimed his, helping him up. "I'll cut you a deal. Give it six months, you foot the bill for a ring, and you're on."

The muscles of his cheeks eased, and he let go of her hands to cradle her face. "Really?"

She gave a silent nod and her heart soared. He rushed to pull her in for a passionate kiss, his lips pressing into hers hard and desperate, the heat of his embrace pouring into her veins and filling her with undeniable warmth. Warmth that offered love and promises.

She didn't want the kiss to end. A kiss she'd spent months dreaming of but never expected. And now she had even more than that. She had him. *All of him.* And a chorus of screams and cheers that came from the front window of her house.

Wait! What?

She disengaged from his lips and turned to find her parents in the front window, the white curtains pushed aside, with Whitney dancing and waving at Laila. Even Chip and Ally were there, grinning at her.

Like her parents had known Ramos would be here and called in extra guests to witness this reunion.

Though she settled somewhere between laughing and crying, Ramos pulled her in again. Totally unaffected by the crowd

"You think you're the only one in need here, Laila, but I need you too." He smiled and pressed his forehead to hers, warming her soul in more ways than he could ever appreciate. "Maybe more than you need me."

He pressed his lips to hers again. Putting on another show for her family. The cheers returned, and this time, she didn't mind so much. Some things were worth celebrating, and nothing could keep her from celebrating having Adrian back in her life.

Epilogue

Eighteen Months Later:

LAILA STRODE into the kitchen dressed in her purple work scrubs. Six months into her new job as a radiologist and she was still very much settling in, with so much left to learn. She loved the challenge and the stable routine, working regular daytime hours at a clinic about a thirty-minute drive from her home.

As expected, Adrian was already in this room, one a great deal bigger and personalized since he'd sold his LA apartment and gone halves with her on a place early into landing her new job. The house stood on the farther edges of Harlow, where she could be part of this town while still a little closer to the neighboring district with its hospital and several medical clinics.

"You look lovely." He made a point of looking up at her, as he plated scrambled eggs for Whitney's breakfast, before he took her to kindergarten, then moved onto his own job working with Blaine. "Come here and let me kiss you."

She laughed and playfully backhanded his bicep but leaned in for a quick peck on the lips, while she also reached past for a piece of toast for the drive to work.

He extended a side-glare, one that said that quick peck wasn't nearly enough. "You better hurry back tonight. Your parents are picking Whit up from kindergarten and keeping her for the night. I can't wait to help you out of those scrubs when you get home."

And that was another thing Laila loved about her new life, not only did her parents have a new home, but Whitney's sleep overs had reduced down to Friday nights only, with weekends open for get-togethers with extended family.

Another good thing? Adrian's new work look. Those button-down shirts and heavy work boots never failed to bring a slow smile to her lips every time she looked at him a little too long.

He'd spent a good portion of the last year fine-tuning his building skills at Oak Tree Furniture and helping with the town's rebuild. Blaine's business continued to grow, and once all the out-of-town construction crews moved on, the town would need people to keep up the day-to-day repairs.

Adrian loved his job. He no longer worked alone and got to spend more time outside in the clear country air. And she loved how much lighter his presence had become from all the new friends he'd made along the way. Oh, and the fact she now lived with a man who spent all day working with his hands...

Her cheeks twitched with a growing grin, just as the *thud, thud, thud* of Whitney's bounding footsteps barreled down the stairs. She wore a pink dress and red leather shoes, ready for kindergarten. Well, except that her dress was backwards and her shoes were on the wrong feet.

Laila chuckled and bent to give Whit a kiss on the head. "Good try there, kid."

"Mommy, can I bring Buddy with me today?" The little girl referred to the six-month-old Beagle puppy they'd settled on buying in lieu of the sibling Whitney kept insisting on.

Laila was so new to her career and wanted more time to just enjoy Whitney without the same pressures that had dogged her in those early years.

"No, sweetheart." She shook her head and wrestled to spin the Whit's dress the right way around. "Your kindergarten teachers are busy enough looking after you and your friends, but Buddy can come for the ride in and say, 'Hi' to the other kids, before Adrian takes him with him to work."

Whitney gave an excited nod and bounced on the spot.

Laila turned back to Adrian and pointed to Whit's shoes. "Can you fix those? I've got to run."

She gave him one last kiss goodbye, and then headed for the door, where the scene of a healing Harlow landscape opened up before her. But so much more than the land continued to heal.

As much as she and her new family loved the occasional sun-filled holiday in LA—with beach visits and time with Adrian's boisterous family—Harlow still had her heart. Besides, Adrian liked the slower pace. Even if the whole syndicate ordeal had taught her to keep those close to her, closer. That this town, like any place, had its flaws.

And speaking of the syndicate, as seemed typical, Rudolph wasn't yet in prison. Like most people with his kind of money, he'd surrounded himself in a fortress of red tape, though at least his credibility was shot, and he didn't have the same influence as before. Meanwhile, a great number of syndicate members farther down the ladder were incarcerated and the organization itself had disintegrated to nothing.

"Laila!"

She paused just as she was about to slip into her open car door, the urgency in Adrian's tone forcing her to turn around. His long strides brought him from the front door in a hurried jog to her side.

"You forget these by the bathroom sink." He extended a hand, and she caught the metallic *ting* of two rings colliding in the palm of her hand.

Her wedding and engagement bands. The wedding ring was made of plain yellow gold, and the engagement ring equally simple, except for a small, oval aquamarine Adrian said reminded him of her eyes.

Though their wedding day had occurred two weeks after moving into their new home, the event had been a subdued affair. That simplicity suited their personalities, as well as the mood around town given how much had been lost. They held the celebration in their yard overlooking the Mirabelle River, the event doubling as a christening of their new place. An expanded homecoming party of sorts. Only close family and friends invited, and Ally acting as Laila's bridesmaid with Whitney as an adorably cheeky flower girl.

Laila pushed the rings back on and smiled up at him. "Always got my back, don't you?"

He pressed a kiss to her forehead, then held her gaze, his dark stare, as always, speaking volumes without him having to utter a single word. Just like Harlow, a lot of things could be rebuilt. Homes and lives. Relationships, too. And as much as this moment right here would have seemed mundane to most anyone else, to Laila, this small slice of ordinary was everything she'd wanted for so long.

So, even as Adrian's lips paused before hers, just a breath away from kissing her goodbye, she closed her eyes and believed him when he replied, "Always."

THE END

JOIN TO GET A FREE NOVELLA AND EXCLUSIVE KATERINA SIMMS MATERIAL

Building relationships with my readers is one of the great joys of writing, it keeps me from turning into a robot! My newsletters are filled with information on new releases, cover reveals, sales, giveaways, and news relating to my series.

To claim your copy simply go to the "Free Book" page on my website.

www.katerinasimms.com

Also by Katerina Simms

For latest releases, go to:

https://katerinasimms.com/books

About the Author

Shortlisted for the International North Street Book Prize, Katerina Simms is a contemporary romance author, who was originally born on a sunny Mediterranean island. She later moved to the weather-challenged suburbs of Melbourne, Australia.

Tea addict, nature lover, and terrible gardener, Katerina's novels feature vivid modern settings and heart-stirring characters, punctuated with the occasional good laugh. Her romances skirt the edges of women's fiction, and her favorite tropes are opposites attract, slow burn, and heat with heart.

www.katerinasimms.com

How About A Review?

Authors love reviews, and good ones help us make a living, and thus write more books! If you've enjoyed this book, please consider leaving a review on Goodreads or your retailer of choice, or sharing with your favorite reader group. Just a line or two would make a wonderful difference!

Eternally grateful,

Katerina Simms